RULES OF THE RED BOOK

Hi Bronwin!
Thank you so
much for the
support! Happy
reading ☺

RULES OF THE RED BOOK

Metamorphosis

Poojitha Tanjore

NEW DEGREE PRESS

RULES OF THE RED BOOK

Metamorphosis

ISBN

978-1-63730-427-3   *Paperback*

978-1-63730-511-9   *Kindle Ebook*

978-1-63730-512-6   *Digital Ebook*

They say it takes a village to write a book. I say it doesn't. **It only takes the love of one's family.**

To Sitamma, my great-grandmother who taught herself to read and write and fought every limit placed on our female ancestors to foster a legacy of strong women, I owe my passion.

To Ushamma and Ammamma, the grandmothers who wove jasmine through my hair during summers in Tirupati, I owe my heart.

To Buji tatha and Amma tatha, the grandfathers who would walk to every temple and the ends of the earth by my side, I owe my determination.

To Hari kaka, Bhargavi aunty, Harish mama, and Manisha aunty, who always let me babble about the work I love, I owe my drive.

To Ananya Tanjore, the young lady I have the honor of sharing a last name with, I owe my childhood.

To my mother and father, your role in my life is too large to be spoken. I owe you both my life.

This book is dedicated to the ones we have lost, both my Amma Tatha and my Kaylan mama.

AUTHOR'S NOTE

———

Welcome to my journey of writing a book about cannibalism and witches as someone who has never had meat and hates scary things.

At the start of 2020, I pulled out my bright-orange journal. In it, I wrote that I wanted to write a book about great love. The main problem was I was nineteen and had never fallen in love. My family has had generations of children and arranged marriages in India. My parents were the first to really fall in love, but they grew up together, and I didn't have anything like that. I had no blueprint for writing about love. So I crossed the idea out and decided to just write a book about something else.

I had grown up as a grassroots organizer for young women in politics. Making speeches about my own narrative to encourage individuals to get civically involved became second nature to me. I continued to ponder what I wanted to write a book about, even if it was only for my eyes. I settled on detailing the narratives of those in politics, often finding joy in conversations with those drastically different from myself. And then I remembered I wanted to work in diplomacy and politics for the rest of my life. Maybe this was the time to have some fun writing out of my comfort zone? I crossed that idea out too. Fun was for people who knew what they were talking about.

Then, I wrote a short story about cannibalism for a creative writing class over the summer. We were told to finish this sentence: "He looked up from icing the last cupcake..." The story could have very well been a wholesome one about baking, but I was dealing with a bout of paranoia from my insomnia and just decided to write what I thought was scary. So it became a story about two brothers in a cannibalistic society.

The kicker was I was vegan at the time and had been vegetarian my entire life. More than that, I have always been a hater of anything scary and creepy.

While writing a scary short story about meat, I learned to write what I did not know. So dear reader, you are reading a book that, six months ago, *I did not know how to write.*

As I workshopped this summer piece, I started to read again. I was devouring a fantasy series and loved every second of it. I had avoided reading fantasy for so long because I had convinced myself it was not conducive to building my professional knowledge. Now I was reading like a child again.

When I was given the chance to write a book, I had finally overcome my need to write about what I was an "expert" in. I rarely enjoyed nonfiction, so I decided I wouldn't write a nonfiction book. This opened up an entire world. As someone who grew up on Percy Jackson, Harry Potter, the Shadow Hunters universe, and more fantasy novels that gave so many young people a passion for reading, I knew I wanted to write a fantasy novel. Beyond the occasional biography and literary fiction book, I pretty exclusively read fantasy. Months went by as New Degree Press approved my idea and I began writing.

I was still so worried the book would be useless. But fantasy was never useless to me, so why was I so worried now?

It was then I realized fantasy had never been just about escapism for me. It had taught me about love, politics, and how to save the world. It had inspired my fifteen-year-old self to speak publicly in front of thousands of politicians to advocate for what was right. Fantasy was my origin story. While I still did not know anything about cannibalism, love, or magic, I knew a lot about how they impacted me.

So why did I write a book about something completely foreign to me? Because I would never stop to correct myself, tell myself I was wrong, or get writer's block by overthinking. Sitting on the brown couches in the University of St. Andrews' Lumsden TV room or in my bright-pink twin bed, I could just write. After long days at school and working three jobs where everything I wrote had to be factually correct, writing my own book felt like home.

Human meat and its consumption could look however I wanted it to in this book. Moreover, the witches and the witch hunters didn't have to follow any guidelines—they are *my characters*! This book is my imagination running wild; the imagination of that little girl who devoured the words of James Patterson and J. K. Rowling in car rides when I was twelve. These words are mine, and I hope you will let them become yours, too.

When I wrote that I wanted to write a book in my bright-orange journal, I wanted it to be about "great love." However, even though I had avoided writing about love in fear my nineteen-year-old self would be exposed for her innocence, this book *is* about great love. It is about meat, horror, and love.

It is also about becoming everything you hate, deep moral conflict, and the hatred we are taught to possess. Through writing *Rules of the Red Book*, I learned about it all. My hope is that, in reading this book I did not know how to write, you will also learn something you did not know.

My hope, more than anything in the world, is my words will make *you* want to write what you do not know.

CHAPTER 1

———

"Keep moving! One foot in front of the next! It's not that difficult!" Mallor yelled at the troop of men behind him. Meant to be matching his pace, they were struggling to keep up as Mallor marched forward with a purpose in each step. Mallor's men wouldn't be destroyed by cannibalism if he could help it.

Two hundred years ago, a desperate camper who had been left alone for months had discovered women turned into witches by eating human flesh. The power was enticing, but it was soon found the same act would either kill his men or debilitate them. That wouldn't happen under his watch.

"Okay, jump boys!"

The troop launched themselves over the edge and into the water, the slap of the cold waterfall burning their faces, all senses overwhelmed by the hollow echo of the waves in their ears. The roar of the waterfall devoured all other sounds. Used to the harsh hit of the water, the troop pushed against the tide, swimming toward the next path on their schedule. Having trained for six months to exterminate the witches, the men were well equipped with navigational competency and pain tolerance.

Mallor, pumping his arms and legs quickly and setting the pace for his clan, swam to the shore and hoisted himself up onto the land. His hands pressed into dirt and stone, creating rough scratches on his palms. Attempting to brush the sand off his clothing, he determined he was far too soaked to continue without changing. Dipping into his tattered pouch, he pulled out a thin gray shirt and a pair of shorts—his last articles of clothing for the trip.

The men, trained to follow Mallor's every move, pulled out their battered bags and began to change as well, many of them sighing in relief as Mallor had refused to allow them to use their last articles of clothing until they were close to their destination.

Mallor laced up his boots and stood up to loop his long, dark hair into a loose hold, wringing the water out. He looked up at his troop.

"They are forty miles north. While we have lost many of our brothers to this cause, I know they dearly await the massacre. The covens will be watching us. We will have to wield our weapons in the most efficient way to kill those women. If you see your former mother, sister, or anyone else who was once dear to you, remember the acts these women have taken part in. They are beasts, and they will take your life with no hesitation. We must take theirs first. This is what we, as men, were bred to do."

The roars from the herd echoed all through the shore and the hills above. They shouted in unison, chatting about their excitement. Despite the long journey, Mallor had trained them in both determination and optimism. While hate for the witches fueled their thoughts, it was the close bond between the troop who had fought with them through witch after witch, giving them an intimidating reputation. Mallor was a god to them, and they worshipped him for treating them as brothers.

"Sir, should we check the map? Just to ensure we can terminate as many witches as possible on the way to the site?"

If a clan member had a suggestion, it had to be directed toward Mallor as a question. He did not accept demands, and you were likely to be stranded to the witches if you slipped up. Mallor responded with a nod to David, his most direct court member.

The Court of Five congregated around a large rock. David pulled the small map out of his back pocket, unraveled it, and looked around the circle.

"The court must decide in which direction we head," he said, tracing the map, his damp sleeve dripping water onto it. "We can head to the village up north, setting us behind a day but allowing our men to rest before battle."

"Why would we bother?" Cell questioned. He was the third highest court member.

A headstrong soldier, Cell could never back down. It made him the best fighter in the clan behind Mallor, but it also jaded his decisions. His election to the court was well earned, but even if he weren't a worthy candidate, he probably would have won as the men feared him. Every man in the coven knew Cell held no regard for their existence beyond what they provided to the strength of the clan.

"The men need to sleep, Cell." Faidor, the court's fourth member, rebutted, knowing he couldn't always prioritize efficiency when he had to do the right thing. "They may have been trained well, but few have the capacity to take on the witches without the strength of night's rest and a meal. Leon can cook once we arrive at the site up north, and I'm sure he's already cleaned the basement in preparation for our arrival."

"So what are we now—bellboys? Leon isn't a clan brother, and he has little grasp of the work we do. It was clear when he was dropped from training in the first cut," Cell barked back at his brother.

Faidor had always had a soft spot for Leon as the two of them had grown close before Leon's incident during initial training. Mallor had told them numerous times not to get close in the first two weeks, as hundreds were eliminated by the second Friday of the training month. Cell knew his brother was weak, but Faidor was also the only one who ever told Cell when he was wrong.

"Cell, this has nothing to do with Leon and you know it," Faidor said. "This is for the well-being of the clan. We have pulled them through the mud for months now with not a single night of shelter or guaranteed food. We can continue on, but you of all people must know even though our clan is trained, they experience burnout. We can't lose this battle.

Mallor pondered. Faidor brought light to the importance of the battle, reminding an eager court of warriors the Coven, the largest in the world, was only to be found together on the East because they were crowning a new leader. The Coven, made up of eight families, had not lost a leader in centuries. The women of the Coven had found with wizardry came immortality, and it was only by the betrayal of one of their own the Witch was now dead.

Her death meant the Metamorphosis was soon. The Election, as it was called in the Red Book, was never meant to occur again. The provisions for the Metamorphosis, however, denoted that the eight families who made up the Coven must all congregate to battle. Each family could nominate one member, praying the member would be granted sole immortality and ultimate power to keep the covens around the world safe from the clans.

The Metamorphosis would be the only chance to end the existence of witches all together. Mallor was dedicated to ending the cannibalism that created witches and the turmoil that was brought about by women realizing they could acquire powers if they ate another human. He raised himself to be a killer and lived off ending the lives of witches, just as they killed innocent humans for personal gain.

As Cell and Faidor bickered, Mallor was jolted from his thoughts by a response from Tate.

"Cell, Faidor, please shut up. You'll end up as barbaric as the witches if you continue like this. We should head east, Mallor. The men can rest; the Metamorphosis isn't for seven days."

Once Tate had spoken, it was decided. The men would head to Leon's in the North for three days, then begin their three-day journey east after they had nursed their wounds and healed.

Tate was the fifth and should have been the least powerful member of the Court. His positioning, however, was by choice. His opinion was the one Mallor had always taken the most seriously, even though Tate was not a fighter. He was a guardian who excelled at finding and killing witches. His predominant role was to care for the men, something Mallor also valued in his leadership.

Mallor looked up from the map and gave Tate a nod.

——

The troops tossed their soaked belongings away. After hearing the news they would be allowed to rest, many failed to hide their relief. Poker faces quickly returned after a scolding from Cell, and the men chatted quietly on the walk to the East.

Trekking through the mud and over the rocks, Mallor grew comfortable with the quick yet sustainable pace of the group.

"How long do we want to spend at Leon's?" Tate picked up a rock and threw it in front of them, keeping his hands busy as he talked strategy with Mallor.

"I was thinking two nights. We don't want the men to quit on us while we're there." Breaks were rarely allowed on the hunt because there was little time. The other reason was, as men got closer and closer to the fight, they historically dropped off like flies. Often realizing they wanted to settle down or find stability, some men found the hunt was not for them. This concept never made sense to Mallor. He ensured breaks were long enough for rest, but short enough to keep the men from deciding to leave.

Tate threw another rock. It landed with a light thud far in front of them. He nodded, agreeing with his friend's suggestion. They rarely spoke about their lives beyond the hunt. They forfeited having a life outside the mission when they were chosen for trials.

Every family with only male children and no relation to the witches was allowed to give up as many of their children as they wished. The children were given to trials at sixteen, and many trained in academies for their entire lives. Each male could be traded for a lifetime of food, and families who gave up all of their children frequently allowed their children to be kidnapped. It was too difficult for the families to say goodbye to their boys, and the ones who did give up all their children already struggled with massive poverty.

It wasn't until the two-year trials were over and the men turned eighteen they were told of the reward their parents received for giving them up. By eighteen, they were already taught not to shed tears. They had forgotten their families had ever existed and channeled their energy into instilling pain into the next class of boys who would never know why their parents forced them to fight the most powerful beings in their known world.

As an only child in a poor family, even without knowing the financial impact his dedication to the hunt would have, the trials were Mallor's only escape. He had been raised on fighting while protecting his mother from violence from his father. The emotional endurance Cell trained the troop for was something on which Mallor was raised. His emotions manifested in physical aggression, and he never yelled for fear of his father. He still did not yell, no matter the idiocy he was often faced with as his troops failed to meet his expectations. He did, however, show the men his disappointment in violence.

Mallor had grown tired of speaking and had fallen back into his own thoughts when he heard the hollow rush of vehicles speeding past. Nearing a highway, he knew they would have to find a way to cross without being spotted by a witch. Highly politically charged, the debate between those who encouraged the women of society to eat others and those who wished to maim them for cannibalism created a polarizing divide between society and the clan.

Halting the men behind him, Mallor spread his arms to keep them from moving further. With only slight stumbles and a few curse words, they stood still, arms to their sides.

"As you men know, we are headed to Leon's." Mallor's voice projected but remained quiet. He did not yell. "However, with the sound of cars ringing behind us, we mustn't go the way of the map. We will reroute, and there will be no questions asked. A single sound in the general vicinity of society could have us all killed."

The silence was necessary, or they would miss his directions. He would hear no complaint of a troop member having misheard him. If you brought death upon yourself through not following directions, your death was self-imposed. They all stood still as Mallor walked to the right side of the troop. Indicating they would be going left rather than straight, the men faced him and began forward once again.

Faidor caught up to Mallor. "Not to doubt your decision by any means, but I do wish to ask how you have found this alternative route?"

"My father took me camping near Leon's when I was younger."

Faidor seemed to understand and did not press the issue further. He nodded and continued forward, trusting him like all the others. Mallor's men moved when he did and stopped when he chose to. If they were following him, his men would never get lost, though they may be killed.

His men felt the many weeks of walking with minimal rest through the blisters on their soles. This was only worsened when they stumbled upon themselves as Mallor abruptly halted.

"Shh. I hear something."

CHAPTER 2

The men went silent, leaving only the wind audible. Mallor tuned in to hear an overlap of footsteps, counting the pairs. Five sets of feet. He began to back up and slowly reached for his pocketknife. If the steps were human, there would be little issue. They would merely have to threaten the group into keeping their mouths shut, ensuring they wouldn't foil their plan to exterminate the witches. While the human world all knew about the Election, very few understood the intricate details of who was chosen and allowed to fight to undergo the Metamorphosis.

If another clan was caught, the men would not have to threaten anyone. However, everyone knew Mallor. He was by far the most ruthless witch hunter, and he rarely slept as he kept an eye out for strangers. If anyone spotted him, he knew they would know someone who wanted to turn him in. The witches promised immortality. The price was high, and he knew to run. It is also why he did not tolerate disobedience.

"Get set," Mallor whispered to his front line and signaled to the rows of men.

Stealthily, aiming to avoid any crunching in the leaves, the clan secured their grip on their weapons of choice.

Hiding the weapons in their jackets or trousers, the men steadied themselves.

"Well, that's what I'm saying!" came a voice. "There is no way Lea is going to win the Election. Not with the Tallaray family bringing in Talea."

Mallor stiffened. The only people who would know details so intricate about the dynamics of the Election would be witches. Despite his instinct to fight, they could not take five witches with as little rest and food as they were moving on. Making a strategic decision, he put his hand in the air, signaling to the men they were to halt. Closing his fist to tell the men to go utterly silent, he hoped through not moving and nearly not breathing, the witches would go by. They stood, breathing slowly through their noses and crouching in even rows in case one clan member tripped.

Mallor peered around, seeing two dark-haired witches with flowers braided into their hair. They were far enough he couldn't make out too many details.

"Wait till Analise gets put up for the Metamorphosis. The Cinder family is trying to negotiate, stating she'll be old enough to compete just two weeks after the Election."

It seemed as if the group had stopped a few meters in front of their men, their voices muffled.

A voice, high-pitched and buttery, rang through clearly as her frustration increased. "They will never go for it. Having to be a seventeen-year-old undergoing Metamorphosis? The pain will stick with her for life. It has never been done before!"

Mallor couldn't help but agree. He had hypothesized that Analise, the strongest fighter of the witches, would be put up for the Election. He had tried not to think about it; his heart yearned for the poor girl to have a childhood. It was obvious hunters hated the witches for being cannibals, but more than that he hated how it turned them all into something they never should have been. He tried to keep his empathy a secret, suppressing it as it only turned him weak with the witches.

Having to kill Analise would sting. Then again, if Analise and her family were choosing to put her up for death, she was ready for it. He straightened his posture and furrowed his brow. If she was being put up to die during the fight to become the Witch, he wanted to ensure her death came at his hands and no one else's.

The witches began moving again, the footsteps distancing. Even though many of the men's legs had fallen asleep from staying still, they moved forward as soon as Mallor indicated they were able.

Mallor's mind was rushing with thoughts about what he had heard. Analise becoming the Original Witch? He knew she would win as he had faced her once and had nearly died. Analise had tried to light him on fire, and he had the burns down his back to prove it. She was ruthless.

———

The fight had occurred three years back. Mallor had just turned sixteen, ranked highest in his cohort, and he was on his first hunt.

"The new one, she is young—only fourteen years old. We expect the Cinder line has been training her since her birth." Teil, Mallor's trainer explained to him as they descended the path toward the Cinder family's village.

He took everything Teil said with the utmost weight, understanding he wanted Mallor to run the hunt. While no one had explicitly told him he had potential, the men trained him for battles and obstacles the other fighters had no access to. Mallor was the youngest individual to ever go on a hunt, being asked to fight before his two years as a trainee were over.

Teil's warning regarding Analise held symbolic meaning. The Cinder family had likely overtrained and overworked this young child because her mother was on her death bed at the time. The death of her mother would leave the entire world of wizardry under attack. Thus far, no one else from the families had been killed. Her mother was fine now, but Analise was always being prepared to take her mother's place just in case.

"So kid, do you miss your family?"

Mallor stiffened at the thought of the family who had abused him and sold him. His mother was a saint, and while joining the hunt was inevitable, it was still not easy to accept his parents did not want him.

"Sometimes," he said. "I miss grocery shopping with my mom and the car rides to school. I always knew this is where I would end up."

"End up? Being here is an honor."

Teil was right. It was a badge of honor to join the hunt and make it through training. However, Teil also did not realize Mallor knew he had been sold. Many of the boys were not told till they were eighteen, but Mallor's father had told him of his fate. The abuse wasn't just physical, after all.

"Mm." Mallor shut back off. Teil didn't need to know he knew the worth he was given. What mattered was proving his worth to himself through killing Analise on this mission. He and his father may not have agreed on a lot, but his father hated the witches, even though many humans stayed out of the business of witches and hunters beyond selling their children or giving up the whereabouts of a hunter for money. Mallor hypothesized it was part of what led his father to maim his mother inches from death nearly every night.

His father yearned for power, and the knowledge that his wife could have more power than him if she chose to commit cannibalism consumed him. He locked her up, tied her up, and made sure there was no way she could be left out of his sight. This abuse had grown regular since the creation of the Red Book, and for this reason, very few women chose to get married.

The pair had begun walking at sunrise. As the sun set, they stumbled upon the Cinder family's village. Streetlights lined the small town, and Mallor grew nostalgic for his home. The lights were glowing fluorescent yellow, illuminating the small shops that catered to witches only. Some shops sold human blood, something many witches developed an affinity for after they turned, despite not needing it. The streets were paved, a characteristic which always caused a sigh of relief in the hunters because gravel revealed their heavy steps. The start of the town was indicated by a large navy sign which had "Cinder Coven" sprawled across in elevated, green letters. The covens never chose to hide themselves. They rarely lost a fight, and even used the arrival of hunters as practice for the young witches.

The air chilled and the sky had grown completely dark. The wind of a late spring night ruffled the map as Teil unraveled it from his back jeans pocket. Furrowing his brow, Teil traced his right pointer finger, nail coated with dirt, across a thin path indicated in blue. Blue meant heavy risk; it indicated past hunters had seen or encountered a record number of witches from the coven along that street. The only time streets in blue were taken by the hunters were when there was enough backup to desecrate the witches.

While Mallor had never experienced the call of a blue trail, he had heard the gossip through little whispers at twenty-minute mealtimes that caused him to wonder. With his big, gray eyes that still sparkled at sixteen, he looked down at Teil. He towered over him at six foot seven, one of the tallest men the clan had seen.

Teil, sensing Mallor's tendency to deliberate over plans even when told to leave it to the better-trained men, turned his head. "What? Never seen the color blue before?"

"No, Teil. I have seen one on a practice training map, but we have never organized it. I have been told even with our entire clan class this year, we do not have enough men to take on a blue trail."

"What you have heard through dining hall gossip with boys who do not yet deserve to be called men should never dictate your decisions during a real hunt."

Teil's tone, belittling the trainees, did not surprise him. Teil never cared for the trainees beyond their logistical contribution to the hunt. Teil's family background was never explained, but Mallor feared it may have been worse than his own. Teil carried himself as if he were made of stone, deflecting any talk of family.

Mallor took a long breath in, preparing for his next question, which would inevitably offend. "How are we to take on a high volume of witches alone?"

"We won't. Taking the weakness and strength of your enemy and using it in your favor is key, Mallor. The double-edged sword of the witches is they have a very short temperament. Both with the human world, the hunter world, and with one another. Despite being family, the smallest tiff will set them off. All we have to do is create a small argument, split the witches up along the blue trail, and take them on.

The blue trail in the Cinder Coven's village is made of the direct family. The original mother, then the six young girls she convinced to commit cannibalism. While the mother is close with her daughters, a history of abuse between the eldest and younger girls continues unnoticed. One of our men witnessed the beating through the window a few months back."

Mallor's vision went fuzzy, recalling moments of hurt and abuse when he was never able to ask anyone for help... He would never wish that upon anyone. But Teil was not taking him on a rescue vision to save the younger witches. He was taking him on a mission in which he would expose the wrongdoings of the eldest child, pitting the mother against her most beloved. That's how it should be.

Shielding his empathy, Mallor let out a remark that would forever feel ashamed of: "Serves them right." He figured if he agreed, Teil would never know the extent of abuse he had undergone. Teil would never question him, nor his ability to successfully kill the witches. He could not have the Court doubting his abilities.

"Truly. Plus, it works to our advantage." Teil's voice had no waiver of lie. He was doing this correctly. "You'll be in charge of bringing the mother to the court steps in five hours. While she is only one, she is also the strongest of them all. You will have to orchestrate a series of events that bring her to the court steps, without ever coming in contact with her or anyone else. The witches cannot know there are men, especially hunters, on the premises."

CHAPTER 3

____

Mallor knew those instructions were the extent of what Teil would say about the plan. He had spent the last year learning the captains often spelled it out for every hunter, painting them metaphorical flashcards to take to battle. It was in the third week Mallor realized he was receiving fewer and fewer instructions before each individual practiced battle.

As he was doing some reading about the history of the Court's creation, he learned the slow decrease in instructions to a trainee only occurred when they were testing for a new leader. Mallor was boggled by the hypothetical nature of this knowledge, but whether the Court was testing him or not, he was determined to be ready for everything.

He began to consider how to expose the eldest daughter's abusive nature to her mother.

"Don't forget to make sure all the sisters are there. We need their echoes to ensure the mother doesn't sit in denial of what her most beloved daughter has done." However, this exposure wouldn't require multiple witnesses. Only the quietest and most passive sister would have to speak up. She would also, due to her personality, be the easiest to manipulate.

"Pass me the map, please." Mallor's use of etiquette was merely to respect Teil. He used formalities for no one else.

"Here, take your copy. The Cinder Coven's main family lives along this street, adjacent to the main street of the village. Their homes are marked with a glowing red C, as all founder families' homes must be. The Red Book also indicates the home of the original witch of the Coven, Helena Cinder, must have a cell to host the hunters who have been killed. The cell is always located somewhere different in each home. Try not to end up there, kid. I'll meet you at the town court steps where you should be prepared to fight. We'll leave from there, so don't lose anything important to you."

The last statement was coated in sarcasm. The men had nothing important on them, both because they knew it would be gone at the end of any fight and because they had nothing. Mallor came to training with the clothes on his back and would die with no other personal belongings. If he were lucky enough, he could potentially pass away with his weapon of choice buried with him. This was an honor, and one he was determined to earn.

"Sounds good. How are you going to get the girls to the court?"

"Who knows?" Teil smirked and walked off.

Mallor should have suspected utter secrecy. It was not only good for protection if he were tortured for information, but it was also in line with Teil's personality.

Mallor smiled in response and nodded as Teil began to walk off. His secrecy was what had brought him so far in the hunter world. He was an enigma, serving as a highly skilled trainer but never accepting positions of power on the Court when asked.

Mallor unraveled the map, smoothing out the wrinkles, and committed the direction he was headed to memory.

There was no way he could run through the village in broad daylight. And even though night had long since come, it was too risky to be a man in a witch's village. He used his uncut nail to etch a path into the parchment that would take him from the outskirts of town.

It was a well-known fact the further out one went from a witches' village, the fewer witches one would encounter. Since the original witch of each clan would live in the center of town near the courthouse, every witch who was not a direct daughter would aim to live as close to the original witch as possible. While the original witch did not possess any real transferable powers, younger witches always treated them as if they did.

Original witches oozed status. There were only eight original witches, and one descendent of each would be eligible for the Election should something happen to the Original Witch. The original witch of a coven could only choose one from their coven to fight in the Election, and so face time with the original witch was invaluable.

Mallor had studied Cinder in history class during training. While the men were expected to train for the physical nature of the hunt for six hours, they were also expected to study strategy. Through history classes, slaving over war strategy problem sets, and presenting each morning on scenarios, he was versed in taking advantage of each family's struggles. Helena was reserved. She rarely left home, and while most original witches hosted their daughters, or direct creations as the hunters called them, in their homes, Helena was adamant each daughter live alone. She erected them beautiful homes, embracing their every want. Magic meant no structure was unattainable. Each daughter could build everything they wanted with the flick of their wrist.

Embracing the chill of the air as the sun disappeared, he took a breath. Gripping the ends of his sleeves, he buried his hands with the folded map under his coat. Mallor remained alert for any witches, but also chose to melt into the little heaven time alone brought him. The last two years of training were brutal for many reasons, but the social exertion of always being around men who were just as burnt out as him was draining. He yearned for comfort in small moments and had especially missed the safety of streetlamps, as none existed in the training camps.

Despite all of his memories with his father being tainted with the sour taste of disdain and the metal taste of blood after a fight, he had missed the walk his father and him would make during Christmas. His street used to be adorned by candles, each family personalizing and lining them vertically until the end seemed nonexistent.

He was brought back to reality as he nearly tripped over broken cobblestone. Walking past a closed store full of blood, his face soured. His mind was so overcome by hatred for the witches who so eagerly killed for their own personal gain, he had nearly missed the small flicker of light in the back of the store. *Nearly.*

Sprinting behind the till, a blonde head of hair appeared in the darkness of the shop. Stunned, Mallor processed the consequences of being caught. His death at the hands of an older witch was almost guaranteed. However, this was his first chance at fighting a witch alone.

Mallor's rash tendencies had gotten him in trouble at home, but it was those very tendencies that garnered him attention and reward at training. Without Teil, he knew this decision could cost him his life or any chance at advancement if caught. It could also lead to his head in Helena's cell. He curled his palm on the metal handle of the door, and tugging failed he used his pocketknife to unscrew the hinges.

Mallor curled his toes to soften the sound of his step and slowly entered the store. A pen fell to the floor behind the till, a small tap of the hardwood floor interrupting the silence. The blonde, small enough to fit behind a counter, must have been young. She would have no reason to hide if she were experienced enough to fight. Unless she was hiding from a witch.

Intrigued, Mallor stepped closer to the till. Silently pulling his sword from the inside of his sleeve, he took off the cap that protected him from being sliced and held it tight to his side. He would reach over the counter, gave the girl a smirk, and put the sword through the very top of her head. Like a pole through her body, she wouldn't be able to survive the pain enough to recover. Her magic would be inhibited.

Not three feet from the till, he sensed her small breaths. In and out. He smiled at the prospect of ending the life of someone who had viciously eaten someone for personal gain. Fueled by the honor this kill would bring him, he put one arm on the desk, propelled himself up and forward, and aimed for her head.

The blonde tuft of hair had, however, disappeared. Baffled, Mallor lost his footing and stumbled as he turned around, surveying the room. Where had the little one gone?

He made eye contact. Her eyes were foggy, tired. Her dirty-blonde hair was in a pile on top of her head, pink pajamas making her the picture of innocence. But the brightness was juxtaposed by much worse signs. Hollow, dark circles consumed her youth, her skin pale . Her gums were bloody and her pretty, green eyes showed signs of a lost self.

In her hand was a blood bag. Her mouth was messily tainted with signs of drinking too quickly. He watched as blood dripped onto her polka-dot-covered top.

He leaped.

The bag dropped to the floor as she pushed a gust of wind out of her fingertips.

Mallor flew back. Stumbling into the shelves of the store, he took in a sharp inhale of air.

"Ugh." As if Mallor were only a mild inconvenience, the short girl shoved a second gust of air. A butcher knife appearing in her hand, she was immediately in front of him. Looking into his eyes, she saw his youth. Smiling like a child with candy, she sunk her knife into his shoulder.

A howl of pain overwhelmed the room. Mallor raged, springing to his feet, using the only power he had: his mass. Tackling her, he brought her to the ground. Not expecting his quick recovery, the young girl took the blow, wind knocked out of her.

On the floor, Mallor on top of her, she pulled her butcher knife from behind her back where it had landed. Staring at him, her eyes showing no sign of fear. She licked the blood clean off the knife.

Shuddering, Mallor remained quiet. Witches were not allowed to kill and eat a human beyond the first human they used to turn. He was in shock.

"There's no way you're getting out alive. Not just because I will relish the feeling of your death, but because I am *absolutely starving*." Her voice was sickly sweet and unwavering. The words coming out her mouth were horrific but coated in a warm syrup; the type that would crystallize into candy.

"Freak." Mallor placed his hand behind her back and flipped her. He quickly moved so he was no longer under her and went for her hands. He was always taught a witch's powers slowed without their hands. Trying to slice the right hand off, blood oozed from her wrist. Her eyes grew wider.

"You are young!" she said and threw her head back, chuckling. "You have no idea where my power comes from, sweetheart." Locking eyes, her face hardened.

A sharp pain began at his side. He winced, reflexively reaching for the cut. Blood coating his hands, he charged at her, using adrenaline to ignore the pain.

Sword up in the air, Mallor didn't know how to fight this. The movement of a hand pushing out magic was the sign he was taught to look for. She could unleash storms just by looking at him, her power unlike any other.

He was on the floor at her mercy. She stood over him, ripping her butcher knife from her back pocket and aiming for his throat.

"Wait! Why are you so hungry?" Mallor was never one to ask questions, but he was hopeful this would distract her.

She stumbled backward, taken aback by the question.

"What? Your life is about to end and that's what you choose to spend your time asking about?"

"Well? You have access to infinite food. Why are you breaking in?"

Her response was coated in sadness. "Access to infinite food doesn't mean I ever end up getting to it."

Her solemn words clashing with her sweet voice caused a pang in Mallor's heart. He pitied her.

"Who's keeping you from eating?"

"Stop prying."

"Maybe I can help you." Although Mallor was planning an escape, he also saw a starving young girl.

"Help me?" She laughed sourly, giving away nothing more than detachment.

"Why are you still talking, then? I don't enjoy seeing someone starve." For the first time, Mallor had hinted at his own experiences. He convinced himself it was not showing weakness, but rather finding an out. If he could convince the girl to talk, he could get her guard down. He would strike then. There was nothing she could say that could make him pity her more than he pitied his own upbringing anyway. She was a powerful witch with a level of power he would never have.

"I have to get home."

Mallor knew he should strike. In a way, her sadness seemed...familiar. He couldn't bring himself to knock her down when she looked frail from hunger. The shelves around him, stuffed to the brim with blood bags and trinkets, fell away as he deliberated what to do.

"Who's at home?"

Both of them sat across from one another, still breathing heavily from the fight before, holding their weapons in their hands. Her shoulders tightened and her jaw clenched.

"Senali. I might be the youngest, but she cares for me the least."

Mallor couldn't believe his luck. He recognized Senali's name as one of Helena's daughters. "What's your name?"

"Analise. Why?"

She was clearly neglected. Mallor could use this to his advantage. Find a way to befriend this little witch who was naive enough to share her name with a hunter. He wasn't sure if he could do it, but he also knew he had to. He was thinking about the reward and the recognition from the men in the clan if he managed to kill the most threatening up-and-coming witch in Cinder. Teil could take the original witch. Together, they would never be questioned again.

Temptation killed him. Swallowing his pride for the plan, Mallor spit the words out. "My father used to send me to bed hungry, too."

Analise's eyes softened. "Oh. I don't remember my human father. We witches do age after all, and I turned very young." Mallor's stomach turned as he recalled what Analise was. He vowed to use his disdain for the witches as fuel for his plan. He was sad Analise's life would end just as sadly as it had begun.

"Why does no one know about what your sister is doing to you?"

"I'm not afraid." Her tone became defensive. "I've never been scared. Only hungry." Her eyes lit back up at the accusation she was weak enough to experience fear.

"I always wish I had told someone about what my father had done to me. My mother always fell victim, but I should have known others would understand." This was a lie. Mallor had always questioned whether the rest of the world would have sympathized with him if he had reported his abuse. More than anything, he wondered if they would respect him.

"There's no chance. I could never report my sister, the woman next in line to be the original witch of Cinder. I would be exiled. They would all say I deserved it."

"Not if you had support. Your sisters must be equally angry?"

Analise sat there in the silence, toying with what Mallor was proposing. "And? So what if they're angry. Five women in fear of the wrath of an original witch are not easy to convince. My eldest sister will be even more difficult to bring along."

"Bring them to the court. If you can convince them to attend, I can get Cinder's original witch. You have my word I won't aim to harm anyone. I wish someone had liberated me from the pain I was going through, Analise. Let me help you."

"I need to eat. If you guard the door right now, I will bring the girls by the court tomorrow at 11:00 a.m. Don't be late. Ensure the original witch is there."

Mallor was being asked to serve as a witch's private security detail as she sucked blood dry from bags and ate it through various puddings. His face went pale and the pit of his stomach churned. He was disgusted by the desire of witches to recall what their first kill tasted like through consuming human blood recreationally. He also knew this was the smallest bargain any hunter had ever been offered in trade for seven kills. Six siblings and an original witch could bring him everything he had ever wanted. No one would dare touch him.

"Okay. I'll guard for you."

Analise perked up. She pointed to the door, then pushed Mallor back into the door through a gust of heavy wind.

"What the hell was that for?" Mallor staggered up against the door, face heating up in shame over what he had let a fourteen-year-old witch do.

"I wanted to see if you'd put up a fight. See if your little hunter pride would get the best of you."

Mallor's lips went taut and his brow furrowed. He stayed glued to the back door, hand gripping the handle. He knew if he let go, he would reach for his weapon. His mind, conflicted between feeling sorry for Analise and hating her, swung between ending her life and sticking to the plan.

———

Analise and Mallor had parted ways at four in the morning. She had run off to bed before Helena woke up, and he needed to throw up. Being around the smell of human blood would make anyone dizzy, but it revolted Mallor as it was mixed with general hatred. With every blood bag she put her mouth around, he felt a little more sick.

Having spent the night sleeping behind a trash can, Mallor missed his own kind. He missed Teil and Teil's faith in him. Analise's ability to humiliate Mallor and his inability to fight back as he stuck to his plan took a toll on him.

Feeling the sunshine on his face, Mallor reached into his back pocket to eat his protein bar. He would begin walking to the court soon. While it would only take Analise five minutes from home to get to the court, it would take him an hour moving from the dark edges of town.

Trekking along and following the path he had etched for himself the night before, Mallor had to trust Helena would be brought by Teil. Teil had never once fallen through on one of his plans, and Mallor knew he would somehow manage to orchestrate a series of events that brought the original witch to the court steps without ever exposing himself.

Mallor hid behind a tree facing into the court. This was the closest he had ever come to this many witches. Faced with the prospect of being killed at any moment with no indication death was coming, Mallor shrunk himself. Hood up, Mallor snuck small glances at the court steps, awaiting the arrival of Helena and the six daughters.

When Analise arrived, Mallor almost didn't recognize her. While her head was held high yesterday, exuding confidence as she spoke with Mallor, it was now her eyes, glowing as they did before, she knocked Mallor off his feet that indicated she was still that same girl. She was, however, scared.

Someone tapped Mallor's shoulder and he jumped. Turning around and smiling with deep relief when he saw Teil, Mallor felt a deep breath provide him relief he had not felt in an entire day.

"Hey, kid. Nice job bringing the sisters to the court. How did you manage?"

"This time around—luck."

"Can't rely on it every time."

"I know. How was bringing Helena here?"

"Also, a matter of luck." Teil smirked.

The two of them watched the Cinder family assemble. Crowds were coming together to praise the eldest witch, all clamoring for the best view of the family.

Analise had stopped shaking since the crowds arrived. Looking as if she thrived off publicity, her head held high once again as she smoothed out her skirt. Prim and put together, the picture of a young girl hiding behind the till of a store stealing food disappeared.

Analise stepped forward. Confusion sprawling across the faces of her siblings, her mother's face remained unphased. Trying not to portray the image of a disorganized family in public, Helena kept her composure in the way only an original witch could.

"Hello, everyone. I'm Analise."

CHAPTER 4

———

The crowd roared. It was obvious Analise was dearly beloved by the other witches, young or old. Mallor knew if Teil was warning him about Analise, word was circulating about how strong she was. He may have experienced her strength in the blood store, but she had revealed emotional vulnerability more than killer instincts.

The sides of Analise's mouth turned up in a smile, smug with the attention she was given. Despite the smile and demeanor with which she carried herself, she was in pain. And more than pain, she may not have been fed that day.

"Today I am here to make an announcement," Analise stated, only a light shake in her voice. Analise's mother turned toward her, eyebrows raising so slightly only one looking for confusion would have noticed. "I am here to propose the jailing of my sister, Senali." The crowd's eyes went wide, many of the witches turning to their friends in shock. "With the Original Witch, my mother, present, I believe the proceedings can begin."

"Excuse me?" Senali said, staring at her with threatening eyes.

Mallor understood this meant, "You'll be hurt for this stunt later."

Analise had to make this successful.

"Mother, please let us tell you the story," Analise said with a begging tone, then looked at her sisters intently.

"We will talk about this in private." Helena's voice raised. "Everyone, return home! This is a discussion between family members. Rest assured, all is okay."

A groan fell over the crowd, all of the witches disappointed they wouldn't see the drama of the family. Helena waved her hands, muttering a quiet incantation.

Mallor realized what was happening and grabbed Teil. Quickly, the two of them launched themselves onto stage, enveloped in the box the incantation created around the family.

Helena had cast a caging spell. Putting herself, her family, and now Mallor and Teil into a contained space to have a conversation on stage where no one could see nor hear. Mallor hadn't fully thought through the fact he was putting himself and his mentor at the hands of a witch family. All he knew was he needed to kill the family, and this would be the only time they would all be together.

The foot-thick box created by Helena began tugging them. As if the box's exterior were made of jelly, the men waded through the caging, hoping to have enough strength to reach the inside.

"What the hell!" Teil's exclamation was slow and distorted as Mallor could just barely hear him.

"We have to fight!" Mallor shouted back, hoping the witches on the inside of the box couldn't hear him. "Ready your weapons! Go for the Original!"

They both knew the Original Witch was the strongest, but also she was the one connected closest to her family. With her dead, the others would be grieving and would also experience decreased powers. There would be a brief moment before they processed Teil and Mallor wanted to kill them when at their most vulnerable.

Traveling through the box sounded like a vacuum. The noise started to quiet. The box spit them out, spitting Teil on his feet but leaving Mallor to stumble into the scene in front of him.

Helena, standing in front of the sisters, was fuming. Analise, directly in front of Helena, was three paces in front of her siblings. Her head still held high, her skin blushed pink as her jaw clenched and eyes watered despite trying to keep strong.

The contrast between the anger she carried last night and the fear that was in her eyes now startled Mallor. He had never been in front of an Original Witch, and it seemed as if the experience would shake even those who were used to it.

Senali stood behind Analise, hands crossed over her chest. She had beautiful, long, dark hair, and eyes that showed no sign of emotion. While her sisters' emotions seemed to display themselves through their eyes, Senali's poker face was impeccable. That, or she was just as emotionless as Analise had painted her out to be.

"Analise, the embarrassment you have caused myself and Senali—" Helena said, cut off by the thud of Mallor and Teil entering the room. "Who—"

Helena had no time to finish her inquiry before Teil shot at her. Honestly, Mallor was shocked they hadn't been seen yet. The family was so caught up in their own drama they didn't bother to survey the room. *How stupid of them.*

The gasps from the sisters came in slow motion, leaving Mallor no time to process the shot taken at the Original Witch of Cinder. While a graphite bullet would not be enough to kill her, she was down. The hunters would have to take off her hands for her to be impaired of power, and consequently easier to kill.

Mallor launched at Analise. She screamed, yet her sisters did not move. Senali, putting up a forcefield between the sisters and Analise, left Analise to die alone at his hand. He was disgusted, yet grateful for Senali's abusive tendencies.

Mallor shot Analise and pounced on her as she was down. He pulled his short knife from his tattered back pocket, grabbed her wrist, so tiny he could wrap his entire hand around it. Her wrist was still raw, and although he hoped his cut from the night before had permanently removed it, he didn't dwell. Creating a cut that mimicked a bracelet, he pushed into her skin, hearing the vile noise of her bones cracking.

Despite the gasp of shock and fear in her eyes, a fire quickly flickered in her pupils. Mallor felt a small drip from the ceiling. Looking up, gasoline was falling onto his face. With a swift wave of her other hand, Analise lit Mallor on fire.

He began to burn, seeing only Analise's cruelty in her expression.

Helena had broken the box, pushing Teil out. She was too weak to fight back, but if she released Teil and Mallor, she could close the box back up. She could shield her children from the hunters, leaving the hunters to fend for what they could.

Teil, risking his own life, reached for Mallor's hand, but Analise pushed a bolt of fire through his chest as both he and Mallor pushed through the box.

Mallor, already flying through, stumbled out and began to sprint.

"Let's go!" he shouted at Teil but felt Teil's hand slip and body go limp. Teil had died from the wound as they left the box. Mallor would have to get out of Cinder, and he would have to do it fast.

CHAPTER 5

Having lost his closest friend and mentor, he would never grow as close with anyone as he had with Teil. The fear of loss was too strong, and as he recalled the events of that day, he was reminded of that fact. The box had dissipated, and Mallor had safely gotten out of Cinder despite the deep burns on his back. Finding his way back to his clan, he had received applause for taking Analise's hand. He did not dare admit he didn't know if the hand was truly severed. He was quickly promoted to Teil's position, a place he felt horrible for taking. He was determined, however, to live up to the position.

"Leon's is just up that hill." Tate's voice jolted him out of reminiscing.

"Perfect. The witches disappeared a few hours back, so I suspect it is safe to move a bit more quickly." Mallor was back on track, ready to get some rest with his clan before his next encounter with Analise. It was possible Analise wouldn't even be the most powerful witch fighting during the Election.

"Sure. Is everything okay? You trailed off in the middle of a sentence and looked a little...gone."

"I'm okay, Tate." A sad smile grew on Mallor's face.

"I know you and Teil were close. I know her name stings. Just because I always wanted to score better than Teil during training sessions doesn't mean I don't recognize how tragic it was to have lost him."

"It wasn't easy when...he was killed. But we continue on. It's what he trained me to do." Mallor had never explained the details of what occurred that day at the court in Cinder. He had never explained the creation of the box and how he could only save himself, ashamed he had left his closest ally.

Tate nodded solemnly. He was the only one who would dare inquire about Teil. "Let's continue up to Leon's. I'm keen for some soup and while that idiot isn't good for much, there's always something warm to eat."

Teil chuckled and patted Mallor's back. The only way they knew to move was forward.

A clan member quickly double-tapped Mallor's shoulder from the back, a troubled look in his eyes. The tap occurred rarely, as Mallor ruthlessly punished false calls that slowed the clan down. He put his hand in the air, signaling they were to stop quietly and place their hands on their weapons.

The clan halted.

Mallor moved forward. He was the only one allowed to move out of formation, and he surveyed the surrounding woods. The leaves were just turning as the summer began to bleed into fall. Had the leaves been dead, denoting each step taken with a loud crunch, the men would be under attack. Not hearing anything, Mallor's face hardened as he readied to yell at the clan member who had slowed the group from getting to Leon's.

Walking up to the hunter who cried wolf, Mallor was stopped in his tracks as the hunter collapsed. Face twisting and eyes going wide, the hunter stopped breathing as soon as he hit the dirt floor of the forest.

"They're here," Mallor uttered the words under his breath, putting his hand up to show the clan to pull their weapons. His men had very little energy, but they would have to gear up. The sixty of them could handle a few witches at high capacity, but their hunger and exhaustion may get the best of them.

A stick fell behind a tree, the noise causing Mallor to jump. He predicted the witches were hiding in the foliage directly in front of them.

Mallor was conflicted. *Do I send my clan charging forward, sacrificing a few lives, or keep them here to fight?*

"Behind the tree!" Cell's comment sent the men into battle.

Mallor's feet moved in autopilot, propelling himself toward the two witches who had revealed themselves. Mesmerizingly beautiful, like all witches, the two women looked startled by the number of men in front of them. He wondered where the other witches had gone, having heard more footsteps. He chose to let it go. Taking advantage of their brief hesitation, Mallor aimed for their hands. With the two of them so close together, perhaps he could remove a hand from at least one—if not both—in one fell swoop. As he neared, the witches removed themselves from their shocked daze.

A strong burst of wind threw him back into three of his men. Realistically, they could have lit the men on fire. Witches were dangerous because there was little restriction to their ability to harness the elements. However, manipulating anything but air exhausted them, and they often stuck to air when they underestimated a threat.

Cell began to take on the witches alongside Faidor. Faidor tied the witches' hands above their heads as Cell made his way through their wrists. A horrific sight, the witches writhed in pain to get out. Tying the women to the tree, Faidor and Cell prepared to hang them.

Gruesome at best, Mallor had grown used to this scene. Cell was ruthless, as one should be when tangling with witches. The women's eyes slowly lost any sign of life, and the tree they so meekly dangled from grew increasingly coated in blood. Mallor watched as it dripped slowly, clenching his jaw and feeling his stomach twist a bit. It happened every time he killed, but it was the cost of doing the right thing.

The witches deserved what they got. It had to be this way, or else the human race would continue to be fed on. If the hunters didn't show a brutal death at their hands would be the consequence of turning, all women would commit cannibalism. They would all seek out power they should never have.

The men applauded and cheered, welcoming the distraction from their fatigue and new injuries. Having had to fend off the witches, all hands were on deck to get the women fully tied to the tree. Even more effort had gone into getting their hands and feet tied together.

As weapons slid back into the holsters, the adrenaline wore off.

Mallor surveyed the area, making eye contact with his men and seeing their excitement fade. Some of their expressions faded into sadness, realizing they had cheered for the lynching of two women. Others' faces showed indifference, having fought and killed too many to even process how they really felt about it all. The latter made up the worst people, but the best fighters. They fought without hesitation and supported their brothers in killing as if they were in the dugout of a baseball game from his high school days.

He continued to survey, making eye contact with one of the younger recruits. Exhausted and sad, the face of a recruit who had seen his first major death was clear. While the clan had seen and caused the ending of many witches' lives over their long trek to the Election, some recruits had never seen the gruesome killing that led clan leaders to exhaustion, fighting to get through the last stretch.

It was time to get the clan to safety and comfort in Leon's home.

Tate tapped Mallor's shoulder, interrupting his conversation with Cell about fighting strategy for the Election. Mallor, intently focused on the map Cell put in front of him, snapped at Tate for interrupting.

"Relax, Mallor. Look up for a second."

He side-eyed Tate. Realizing this response was exactly what made Tate so valuable, he stopped tensing his jaw and allowed his shoulders to relax. Before looking up, he smelled the waft of pumpkin soup. The scent of fresh bread wafted through the air leading to a little, yet noticeable grumble in his stomach.

"I only tolerate your interruptions when they are followed by food," Mallor said.

Tate smirked as the two climbed just a little bit faster up the small hill upon which Leon's house stood.

"So we're clear? We seek to kill the eight, but not all at once," Cell clarified the plan once again. "We kill the last two witches standing at the same time to consolidate."

"Please let up already. You've been talking about this for ages now!" Tate was eager for rest and food rather than fighting strategy.

"Shut up, Tate. It's not my fault you don't know how to plan a fight. There's a reason you don't sit in the top three," Cell barked back at him.

Mallor rolled his eyes and sighed. "You're both idiots."

Despite the fact both men were older than him, he knew Cell was full of it. No one on the Court knew Tate chose not to take a higher position. They always assumed because he was lower in the training scale when they were younger he had not been asked. Mallor had, however, asked him to stand in Cell's position ages ago. Cell looked like a fool, and Tate looked like an irritable idiot for showing impatience. The two would begin their squabble again when Mallor wasn't looking.

Tate was the first to knock on Leon's door. Knocking seven times, four heavy and three light, he signaled they were not intruders. The clan was down to forty men, and they eagerly awaited Leon's home despite the imperfect conditions. The home, left to Leon by the parents he hadn't heard from in years, was charming. Cozy, with dark-green carpets and beige ceilings, the home looked like one that would never belong to a former fighter. Leon had always been softer and seemed like more of a caregiver than a hunter. While many of the hunters went on to be both if they left the clan, Leon was always only one. He lived to take care of those around him, which is likely the reason he failed out of hunter training.

The door swung open, lightly creaking as the latches showed signs of rust as the fall bled into winter.

"Boys! How are you all, then? Come in, come in!" The air was nearly knocked out of Mallor as Leon rambled and embraced him. Clearly thrilled to have any sort of human interaction, Leon urged the men into his home, guiding them all to the basement where they could sleep.

The morning sun disappeared as the door shut, Mallor ensuring all his men got into the home.

The stairs felt as if they could crack on the way down, but no one cared as Leon posted the shower schedule on the back wall, having used the list of names mailed to him earlier by Tate. A filthy mattress covered the cement floor of the basement, large enough for all of the men if they slept feet to head, snuggled up. They couldn't care less, each clamoring to check their names on the shower list. Leon had an outhouse of four showers, and the men would alternate through the day. Each would grab their bowl of soup and bread as they exited the shower after five minutes maximum.

Cell and Mallor had gone back to discussing war strategy on the couch, this time joined by Faidor as he soaked his bread in his soup before answering every question.

Faidor was unhappy with Cell's suggestion to take out five of the nominated witches before the Election. He believed it would cost the lives of too many hunters, leaving only a few to fight the strongest witches. Mallor agreed they would need the most manpower to fight the final two witches. It was clear Cell just wanted the praise that would result if he managed to be part of the few who defeated the final two witches. Sometimes his ego got the better of him, and Mallor would have seen that if exhaustion hadn't clouded his mind.

As the argument escalated, Cell's rant was interrupted by Leon. Slightly jittery, even nervous, Leon plopped himself on the coffee table in front of the three men. "So how have you all been? Big journey ahead of you! I'm so happy you all are here safe, although it looks like you've lost a few."

He was known to have little tact. Bringing up the death of clan members so casually was wrong, but Leon meant nothing by it. An awkward silence followed his rushed rambling, and Cell went back to looking down at his map.

Knowing he wasn't really planning, but merely waiting for the silence to clear up, Mallor spoke. "Yes, sadly we have lost a few men. That is how this profession works, though. We appreciate you taking us in, Leon. I know we were all feeling the fatigue, even if we are sometimes too wrapped up in the next step to admit it."

Leon chuckled. "Indeed. It is the hunter's way of thinking about what is next. I am glad you sat down for a minute. It looks like the rest was needed."

Faidor nodded, then smiled. While he had an aggressive bone in his body, he had a soft spot for Leon. All the men did. Leon was good enough and was one of the sharpest strategic minds in his cohort. However, he lacked competitiveness. He was far more about comradery than climbing the ladder of the clan. You had to be willing to step on others to move up in the ranks, and Leon was never willing to do so. And, for the men who had lost that part of them, he won them over through some incredible pumpkin and squash soup paired with home-baked bread.

For the next three hours, Leon's jittery energy dissipated as the men caught up, telling stories of their day in the same cohort. Rambling away and laughing over tea which eventually turned to beer, Mallor felt a sense of ease which he had thought he had given up forever. Leon was a great host; there was no arguing that.

"So Mallor, have you heard from Teil? My sister has been out looking for him since the news came back."

"Heard from him?" Mallor said. "Leon, he's dead. It's been a few years."

"I didn't even think to tell you earlier! How long have you all been on trek?"

"Four months. Wait, *what* haven't you told us?"

The men all looked at Leon in confusion.

The rest of the clan had long since gone to bed, and knowing he was slightly tipsy, Mallor refused to believe Leon's statement.

"Around two months ago, we got a message from Cinder—an escaped human. They think Teil may still be alive in the basement of Cinder's Original Witch."

"Helena? They never would have spared him. Not after I took Analise's hand."

Mallor couldn't see straight, his arms going numb and limp by his side. His stomach turned, feeling physically sick, and his mind clouded by thoughts.

"There are rumors Helena put him in the basement after the fight. He could very well be as dead as we thought he was, but all we know is he was alive when you got back."

CHAPTER 6

———

"Mallor?"

Cell tried to bring him back to reality, calling his name in an attempt to snap him out of his shock. Mallor had always appeared scary. His dark hair and dark eyes lead to a face that rarely wavered from anger or indifference. The men had never seen him at a loss for words.

Mallor, sitting on the light brown couch of Leon's home, felt like he had seen a ghost. He was imagining someone he thought could only appear as one.

"Teil is alive?" His voice, small and shaking, left a worried expression on Tate's face.

Tate placed one hand gently on Mallor's shoulder, causing him to jolt ever so slightly. "Could be. Remember, Mallor, this news is old. And you know any news we hear about a clan member, their whereabouts, and well-being could change an hour after it is spread. You can't trust it."

Mallor shut his eyes and took a deep breath. "But if he's in Helena's cell, he could be in a lot of pain. He's the one who told me to make sure I didn't get put in there! He wouldn't even tell me in detail the stories he's been told." He had turned into a babbling child, frantic for news.

"You forget I was with him when he was briefed for that hunt! *If* he's alive, he would never let us go get him. And for good reason! The Election is soon, and we need everyone to kill these bastard witches. *Everyone* includes you."

"You're being selfish." Mallor knew he sounded irrational. He hated taking a tone with Tate, but he was frustrated and unsure what to do with his anger.

"It would be selfish of you to go on a mission to rescue one man."

"As if he's *just one man,* Tate! You forgot how important Teil was to the clan. If we could bring him back, we would win the fight on the day of the Election."

"What? So you don't think we can win as we are?"

Mallor clenched his fist and sighed. He needed to watch his next words carefully. It was already hard for him not to speak highly of Teil around the Court, as they all knew Teil would replace any of them in a heartbeat. Only Teil's desire to stay out of the spotlight and his passion for teaching kept him from being a deeper threat to the men on the Court. He may not run the clan if Teil were still around, but he would rather have Teil there. He wanted to give up the fight, go back to his first friend and mentor. His heart pulled him to save Teil.

"That's not what I'm saying. While Cell is an incredible trainer and leader, we could always use another. We need the aggression Teil brings to the team!"

"I'm—I'm so sorry for bringing this up." Leon stuttered, clearly trying to shrink himself as Tate and Cell glared daggers at him for ruining Mallor's focus on the Election.

"Hey," Cell said. "I know you don't want to hear this, but he's more likely dead than not. If Helena got wind of the fact some hunters knew Teil were still alive, she would kill him in an instant. She doesn't want hunters in Cinder, and no hunters should be going before the Election. We have a job to do. These are the sacrifices we make." Cell was not one to chime in on discussions led by emotions. Whether he was worried about Mallor showing signs of weakness or truly felt his hurt, the group didn't know.

Cell was right. Mallor needed to get on the same page as his Court, especially if the two commanding officers who rarely agreed with one another chose to be on the same page. So of course, as any mature individual does when they see the wrong of their ways, Mallor shut down.

"Hey! Listen to me," Tate said and put his hands on Mallor's shoulders, looking him in the eyes. "The Election is only a month and a half away. We will get Teil immediately after. I promise."

Promises were rarely made in the clan. Men so often died before they could keep their promises, discouraging men from making them.

Tate must have had deep faith they would win the fight against the witches, the ultimate hunt, if he was to make a promise of that weight. Mallor glared at what he had said, knowing he was right but refusing to stomach leaving Teil out there for longer. Mallor shoved him. Tate landed on the coffee table, knocking over the pints that Leon had set out.

"Maybe you should get some air, son," Cell said, his kindness coming and going in an instant. His voice now cold, commanding. Looking at the front door, nodding his head in that direction, Cell's suggestion was more of a demand. He wanted Mallor to get out, and he wanted him to do it now.

This discussion was over.

Tensing his jaw, Mallor carefully picked up the shards of glass that remained. "I'll clean it up when I get back."

Leon nodded slowly, watching as Mallor shoved on his boots and coat, clunking out of the house.

The big, wooden door shut behind him, and the lock clicked from the inside. He began to walk, embracing the chill of the night when he nearly tripped over a rock stuck deep in the ground.

Wrapping his fist around the cold rock, he yanked it from the dirt and struck a tree many meters ahead. He set out for a sprint. With only the desire to get as far away as possible from a team who refused his right to bring his oldest and dearest friend back to the hunt, he propelled himself forward.

Betrayed. The word buzzed around his mind, amplified with each step he took.

He closed his eyes, the wind hitting his face and causing his eyes to tear up. Or maybe he was really crying. He didn't care to differentiate, knowing the pain of both would feel the same.

After running for over an hour, Mallor stopped at a lake. Sitting by the brook, he placed his head in his hands. Unexpectedly, he began sobbing. Shaking, hands folded in his lap cradling his head, he couldn't recall the last time he had really cried.

He had deemed sadness a futile emotion, one he couldn't channel into anything. Anger taught him to fight, and joy was experienced so rarely he didn't need to push it away. Sadness, however, he needed to grow indifferent to. Otherwise, he would spend every day devastated by the cards he'd been dealt in this life.

Mallor finished sobbing, his head throbbing from dehydration and a headache. Having run straight, he knew he could get back to the house when he needed to. The men still had another night at Leon's, so he figured he had time to collect his thoughts. To be the leader the clan needed for this next hunt, he would need to be in the right mind. If he wasn't, not only would he hate himself for letting himself down, but Cell would kill him for sabotaging the fight.

The men were always responsible for their own emotions. While a select few, like Tate, managed to keep feeling and cope with a myriad of emotions in a healthy way, most of the clan turned off their ability to feel. Mallor had chosen the latter for himself, and it had worked for years. It would work again. He just needed some time to himself. The Court and Leon could handle the clan. After all, they would just be stuffing their faces and falling asleep.

Mallor decided he would walk until he processed his sadness. He had never known how to process grief and loss, mostly because the only loss he had ever experienced was of his parents. While he missed his mother at the start of his training, if he entertained every thought about her, he would be filled with guilt. Thoughts of his mother would only lead to thoughts of his father. While he initially sought out thinking of his father because it would bring him the anger he needed to fuel great fighting, he quickly learned dwelling on his past abuse only led to unresolved feelings of shame that came with trauma.

Feeling for the map in his back pocket, he held it in front of him. While it was dark, his eyes had adjusted to the color of the night enough to mark his location. He wouldn't walk too far; he would need to be back by midday tomorrow to lay out travel plans. He also wanted one last warm shower before they headed out for the next month or so.

After a few hours of wandering, Mallor's heels throbbed. While the first two hours had brought him necessary intro-spection and settled his spirits, he had spent an hour or so seeking a place to rest. He intended to wake up at five in the morning and spend about four hours making his way back to Leon's. While he had deemed himself one who did not care for special experiences, he had a sudden urge to see the sunrise and appreciate it. Maybe he was just going insane as he would soon run out of water.

Sighing from exhaustion, he found two trees that had fallen. Their trunks had crashed into one another, crossing diagonally, and forming a bridge of sorts. The trunks were wide enough to hide him if he needed time to react to an attack. He could rest there and pray it wouldn't rain. He nestled his head onto a pile of leaves, crunching as the fall weather had dried them. Stretching out under the tree, Mallor shut his eyes.

He hoped not to dream of Teil.

CHAPTER 7

——

As he slept, the sight of Iro Coven appeared behind his eyes. Known for being the last addition to the original families, Iro's youth showed in its architecture. Most coven's villages mimicked old Roman architecture. Following the classical precedent set by the Greeks, Roman architecture allowed the witches to feel powerful. They were the closest to mythological beings the world had ever seen and wanted the world to know the power they held.

Often seeking to play god in their early days, the witches tore society apart as they learned the extent of their powers. As more women became witches, rules were set by the Original Witch, as she knew peace had to be established before hell was unleashed on earth.

The *Red Book* denoted the rules for witch jurisdiction and power use, using its hold on the community to run everything. The book had never been seen, but it was trusted that it lay with the Original Witch. When she passed, provisions were made for the passing on of the book. It would be held by the witch who won the Election fight, but until then, it sat with whoever it was left to by the Original Witch.

No one knew who was chosen, as they had to keep it a secret. The rules of the *Red Book* were widely spread through various copies, but the Original Witch had always held her copy dear. It didn't hold any real power, as far as the hunters were concerned.

Mallor's dreams were painted with the streets of Iro. Ice cream stores, blood banks dyed blue to match Iro's colors, and classy restaurants lined the main street. The village was almost welcoming. It wasn't until one saw the cups and bowls filled with human blood that a person's heart fell into their stomach. Iro, the quintessential youngest sibling, took what they wanted when they wanted it. They were reckless, and they consumed the most amount of blood. Their creator, Lyssa, had turned and been hungry ever since.

A few months after Teil's supposed passing, Mallor was sent into Iro on his first mission with Cell. The *Red Book* denoted the witches were not to kill for their blood storage or food needs. There were two types of humans willing to donate blood: men strung along by a witch for whom they had fallen hard, or women who were looking to turn into a witch.

Mallor would always see donors as horrible people. *Scum of the Earth, supporting the witches.*

The first few original witches had suffered through transition alone, a process rumored to be more painful than childbirth. So they created a system. If a woman could prove her devotion to one of the eight original witches, they would have a safe place and comfort to turn to. The original witch who accepted them would even help them find a human to eat to trigger the turn.

Soon enough, families emerged. Iro was reckless, and women seeking the acceptance of Iro and any other coven would have to donate so much blood they could die. Many did die.

However, a year after the venture into Cinder, it seemed as though Iro broke a crucial rule of the *Red Book*. They were killing humans, as they did not have enough blood in the stores. Once the clans were told, many along with Mallor's clan were sent to fight. He was only a year from promotion to head of the clan from Teil's old position, and his time with Cell was his final test.

While his dreams did not provide him the exact details of their trip, he recalled the loneliness. After a day weaving through the village nearly mirroring the way Teil had ordered him to do in Cinder, Mallor had grown tired of Cell's chatter. He loved to discuss strategy, but Cell was droning. Mallor couldn't remember what he said, but he'd suggested the two split up to continue their killings. They had quietly executed nearly a dozen of the youngest witches of Iro, but had more work to do. Mallor would get his quiet and they would be out of Iro soon.

Mallor, having killed thirteen witches without the partnership of Cell, had sat to rest behind a tree. Smelling similar to the forest he was sleeping in now, it was almost as the two places had blended into one.

A slew of killings later, he was exhausted but equally exhilarated. It was only when the sun began to set and he knew he was to meet with Cell out front of the town entrance he began to settle. His hands had stopped shaking and his breath had slowed. Leaning against the cold tree trunk, he realized this was his first moment of silence.

While he often completed missions by splitting from his counterpart to cover more ground, he often fought until the last second of the mission. Iro, however, seemed to be so populated and so cluttered with blood it was rare anyone noticed a witch disappearance. Iro was also far less organized than the other covens that Mallor had visited.

None of the witches seemed to spend time fawning over the Original Witch of Iro, meaning they were far less civilized and elegant. They were free spirits, and often very young. This led to something of a perpetual late night college town energy that enveloped the streets.

The few moments Mallor had snatched from the day had given him silence he hadn't experienced since sitting on his bed at home moments before his father came home from work. Sitting there, he finally processed the grueling training he had been put through this last year.

At eighteen, he had climbed the ranks of the most intense clan training in the world. Moving more quickly than many of the leaders did at his age, he was feared by his peers for his brutality and feared even more so by his superiors as they felt threatened. He thought about the time his bunk mate had tried to push him off the balcony that overlooked the training area, and the fear he'd felt, but recalled even more the adrenaline that rushed through his hand as he threw his bunk mate off the edge.

The shame he was destined to kill was overpowered by the joy of having found his calling at all. Years of taunting at school and by his parents for being subpar at academia had eaten away at him. Knowing he could end someone's life gave him power. He was applauded by the clan elders for taking matters into his own hands and was respected by his peers for claiming the life of someone who could be malicious out of envy. Envy was the fire that burned through the clan trainees, motivating them. One had to handle the emotion well or become consumed by it.

He further recalled the sleepless nights followed by early mornings. Men were denied showers even when covered in blood and sweat after just mere hours of training. There were days his hair would mat, becoming disgustingly coated in dried sweat and mud that had cemented from outdoor training. Coming from a father who would scold him for being unclean, he was plagued by his father as his inner monologue. While disgusted, he was always a bit proud of the grime under his fingernails as he knew it would piss his dad off. Sleep in itself was difficult, both before and after his bunk mate had passed away. He had tossed and turned on his hard mattress, anxious energy after a long day exacerbated by the fear he felt for missing his alarm in the morning.

He knew the potential he had to become a great clan leader. As a boy from a poor family with little academic talent, he finally felt like he had a chance for a great future. He had never had anything to lose but was now highly aware of the fact he could lose his only chance at pursuing a calling.

Between the anxiety, paranoia, and desire to be great, Mallor grew more and more comfortable with a lack of sleep. The deliriousness that used to set in when he didn't sleep long enough quickly became part of his identity, leading him to accept the cruelty of the coaches and shake off injuries in fights as if he healed on the spot.

Recalling the events of being in Iro and the roots of the loneliness and anger with which he carried himself now, Mallor drifted off into a deep sleep and only stirred when a cold gust of wind came across him. As hours passed dreaming, sometimes even blessed with a joyful memory from training, Mallor enjoyed rest. Despite the inconsistently peaceful nature of his rest, it was the closest to ease he had felt in a long time.

At the point where dreams blended into reality, Mallor flinched upon hearing a noise. Unsure if the sudden and loud rustle of leaves was from Iro coven in his dream or from the woods he was asleep in, he groaned and tried to ignore it. He had long craved rest and wasn't ready to give it up for the crunch of a few leaves.

His eyes shot open at the sound of breathing. Pushing himself out from under the trunks, he stood up. Seeing no one, he quickly looked around his surroundings. The woods, lit by the smallest light of a rising sun, looked as they did when he had fallen asleep. Thinking the breathing had been from a character in his dreams, he mourned the sleep he had lost to his anxieties. Accepting he should just start walking back to Leon's, Mallor bent over to collect his bottle of water.

Not just hearing the breathing this time, but feeling it above him, Mallor sat up and whipped his knife out of his back pocket, whipping around with his arm outstretched. Air swiped against his wrist, knocking his knife out of his hand.

Upon seeing bright, green eyes in front of him, he realized he was unarmed against a witch. As he patted his pocket down and tried to find his sword or a gun, he realized they must have been taken from him as he slept. Normally a light sleeper, he must have lost himself in a moment of silence to himself. He would be fighting against this witch alone.

He had trained for this. Every week, the men would be forced to fight barehanded against someone with weapons, to simulate the disadvantage hunters had when fighting without one. More than preparing them for this situation—because fighting a witch was unfathomable until one did it—it made men protective of their weapons.

Quite frankly, he was tired from fighting. The encounter with the witches in the woods had thrown him for a loop, and all this thinking about the past had taken up any energy he had left.

Fighting, however, came most naturally to him. Having climbed the ranks during training in a constant state of delirium, he shook off the lack of weapons. The woman in front of him, green eyes and short brown hair, was captivating. He stuck his leg out, trying to hook it behind hers. As he began to defend himself, it was as if time stopped. His motion slowed, his legs moving as if they weighed a thousand pounds. She swung at him at lighting speed and he flew back, hitting the ground with a thud. She walked over. No magic used, she merely kicked him in the head each new blow causing the blood to ooze just a bit more. Slumping back, he counted three kicks before he began to spin. Four kicks before he stopped trying to get up. Five kicks before his sight went black.

CHAPTER 8

———

Groaning, Mallor woke up with a throbbing in his head. Under the sun, he lay in leaves and dirt. Mud stuck to every part of his back. Mallor felt paralyzed. He lifted his finger, tried to flip to his side, but pain soared through every part of his body. He closed his eyes again to see a purple and blue tint. Seeking to find solace in sleep, he tried to nod off, but tensed when he remembered he had to return to Leon's. *The clan!*

They would be off by now. Mallor had taught them never to wait for someone unpunctual. He had intended for the statement to be a lesson, but the men would follow the rule. Cell would ensure it, no matter how much he might miss Mallor.

Maybe they would come.

Maybe they would find him.

He had to have faith the court would come. How much time could have passed? The men might not have even left for the Election yet. Or they would leave soon.

Mallor was determined to get back to Leon's. Stumbling up, he scraped the mud off of his back as he could reach. He began to tip, stretching his arm out to lean on the tree trunk behind him. Touching the trunk, he found blood. It couldn't be his. There was far too much of it.

Panicking, he touched the top of his forehead and winced. There would be more damage. He touched the back of his head, just at the crown of his scalp. Hardened blood. Parts of the wound were still wet and healing over. He was shocked by the surface area of the injury, but grateful that the wounds seemed to be scabbing. He had a concussion, and was suspecting a contusion, too.

There was no chance he'd make it back to Leon's. Before he could find a solution, green eyes stared upon him. Grabbing the tree trunk for support, he inched his way to the side. His vision began to blur, but he was determined to escape. All he saw was her hair, just the side of her face peeking out from behind the tree a few meters in front of him. Her eyes followed his, and there was no escaping them. Her hand flicked from behind the tree and he felt the repercussions as he fell over.

His vision went black again.

———

The sun was at its peak. The weather was brisk, a wind brushing across him and making his whole body shiver. His eyelids stuck, opening slowly as if it had been ages since he had used his vision.

Maybe it had been. Mallor had lost track of how long he spent laying in mud. The girl with the green eyes hadn't bothered him lately, and he was hoping it would remain that way. He surveyed the woods as best as he could without straining his body. No one. It was possible she had left. She *had* to have left. He couldn't withstand much more of this torture. The constant blacking out was horrific, and he was painfully dehydrated. More than hurt and dehydration, hunger dominated his thoughts.

He held out hope he could return to Leon's. While the men might have left already—although he still hoped they were out looking for him—Leon would still be there. Just the thought of warm soup and bread gave him the motivation he needed to stand up.

Hesitant and moving very slowly both out of caution and need, Mallor pushed himself off the ground. He hoisted himself up, shutting his eyes as he winced. As the hardened mud fell off him and he dusted leaves off his pants, he was overjoyed not to see the witch with the green eyes. Rolling his shoulders back, he fixed his posture and found his knife a few meters away. Cursing himself for not having found it sooner, Mallor was also thrilled he now had a weapon. There was a lot he could do with a knife if necessary.

He was getting distracted. Mallor set foot forward, digging his map from his back pocket, determined to orient himself and get back home by the end of the day. It had taken him less than half a day to get to this godforsaken part of the world, and it would take him just a bit longer to get back. He could eat, get patched up, and make his way toward the Election.

He had always hated the witches but had lost his fury through guiding the men. He got lost in the mission, and after being nearly killed by the witch who had kicked him over and over again, he was seething with anger. At least he knew where to channel his anger. He had less of an idea of what it felt like to be lost. Even at his loneliest and most hurt at home, Mallor found solace in knowing he was with his mother.

The clan had since given him a sense of community and he rarely felt lost, no matter how low in the ranks he had started. He hadn't had a moment to himself since that day in Iro, sitting behind the tree. Oh, how he wished he was still in the dream. He caught himself from going down a dangerous rabbit hole of thoughts, not ready to wish death upon himself yet.

He would replace all this thinking with action. It was time to move. It had been time to move for days, the loud grumble of his stomach and scratchy state of his throat confirmed. He wanted to try and trace back time and looked intently at his map, tracing his steps. He had left Leon's home, taking around six hours to get to where he was.

Since all the clan men were taught to walk at the same speed, he thought it would only take him a few hours to return home. He assumed he had taken his time getting here without the clan, and might even be slower now that he was injured. He was likely over twelve miles from home. His new injuries would inhibit him, and he would inevitably need breaks.

He recalled the stream he sat by on his walk over. Fortunately, the men always carried a water filter as a byproduct of constant travel. It had come in handy these past few months on the hunt but would prove invaluable now. All he needed was a body of water. The stream was three hours away and was the closest one he could remember. It was also the only access point listed on the map that wouldn't be a detour.

Forward was the only way he knew how to move. He began his walk and heard nothing for three hours. As the sun began to fall, but not nearly set, he thanked the skies for having rid him of the witch's company. He sought to lose himself in memories, to forget the pain his head injuries sent through his body. The searing throb in his head had forced him to puke three times since leaving. The puking was unhelpful, and he no longer had any food in him left to keep down. He was getting desperate for something to eat.

Just as he was losing himself in thought about previous missions, strategizing ways he would help the clan win the Election hunt when he got here, a deer appeared just meters away. Trees rustling, both Mallor and the deer stopped. The deer, elegant with its antlers raised high and deep brown hairs, stared back.

Mallor, on edge from expecting the witch to return, was shocked by his luck. He could eat this deer, and he had a knife that would help him accomplish the deed. Its eyes widened, as if understanding his murderous thoughts. Mallor knew he would have to chase, and the spike of adrenaline that came from killing fueled his motivation. While his head might hurt, his legs still worked, and his years of training through pain would provide him food.

The deer began to walk, seemingly unphased by Mallor's existence. Maybe it sensed his exhaustion. Either way, Mallor took advantage of the slow movement, lightly jogging to keep up with the long strides of the deer. The sounds of its footsteps were rhythmic, and almost gave him some relief from thinking about the disaster he was in. *Thump, thump, thump…* The tap of the deer's hooves led to Mallor's calculation he would have to walk at double speed. He was able to keep up, but not close enough to throw his knife without scaring the animal off.

The thumps began to speed up. Mallor began to sprint. This deer was his last bit of hope. His stomach yearned for food, and he needed something to prove it would all be okay. He needed something good right now. He chased, exhilarated and thankful his legs still worked.

Mind entirely focused on the mission, he pumped his arms to kill this deer as if it were the witches at the Election. Nothing could stop him from ensuring the death of the other in either situation.

Mallor felt in rhythm with the deer, widening his stride as if he were suddenly the fastest person in the world. In his enjoyment of the chase, his grumbling stomach was overshadowed by his quick breathing. He had worried he would never have a goal again, and this gave him not only something to run away from but something to run toward.

The deer stopped and turned. Its eyes flashed green. It was as if Mallor could hear it laughing at him as he caught his breath and pressed his temples. The toll that running had taken on his concussion was painful. He clutched his knife, raising his arm ready to throw it, and the deer sprinted away. This time, its speed was nothing Mallor or any other human could have caught.

Exasperated, Mallor's knees collapsed under him. Still breathing heavily, he wept, lost due to his failure to kill the deer. He put his head in his hands and tried to scream but was interrupted by hiccups.

He looked up, wiping his eyes. The hiccups stopped. His breath hitched.

In front of him lay a dead body.

His heart fell into his stomach. His brain spun. He had seen a dead body before, but not one nearly this maimed. The body was covered in gashes. *Don't throw up. Don't throw up.*

The sight was horrific, but he thanked the universe the body had not begun to smell yet. Its eyes were still open, mortifyingly looking out into nothing. It lay there, ironically, in corpse pose.

Mallor hypothesized it must not have known its death was coming, otherwise it would have shut its eyes in anticipation. *It.* What an odd thing to call a human. *It* looked female, with long lashes and choppy hair to the shoulders.

He grieved for her. He grieved for himself. He'd lay there dead with her soon. With no energy to keep moving and the sureness he'd die of hunger on the journey, Mallor was exhausted.

An idea struck him.

The mere thought of what he would do to save himself caused his head to spin. Caused his stomach to spin. Somewhere between the teetering nausea and unease, his body vomited. The last bit of fluid splashed across the floor. The vomiting had only aggravated the urgency of his hunger problem.

Through his groaning, only one thought came through. *I need food.*

He needed to cut into the woman that lay in front of him. He knew from stories of men who had attempted to acquire magical powers no man could turn. No man would ever become magical, and he at least wouldn't become the one thing he stood starkly against.

Mallor's head still throbbed, painfully sore to the touch. *Maybe my judgment is clouded.*

No. I need to survive this. I need to make it back for the Election. I only ever had one calling, and I'll be damned if I give it up now.

His face heated in shame as he thought about eating an innocent human. He was also deeply afraid to be found out; men who committed cannibalism never found powers, but always risked the chance of dying. Many men were so adamant they could become the first wizard, they risked their lives in waves. Groups of men, just like the clan, would train for months to eat people—training to survive the transition—something they only knew of through passed down stories and rumors.

If I die and am found here, lying next to a dead body, I would never be remembered for anything else. He couldn't stand the disrespect that would come with being found dead after having tried. It was like diving headfirst into death. But, so was doing nothing. All Mallor could fathom was his hunger. He was taught to survive, and while it had always been in pursuit of witch desecration, his instinct remained. He would never tell the men, and he would dedicate his life to redeeming himself through leading the men into the Election.

His hands, shaking, dropped the knife. Perhaps a sign not to commit this atrocity. *No.* If he talked himself out of this, he stood no chance of living. His throat dry, Mallor tried to swallow.

He bent over and steadied his hand as he grabbed his knife. Standing up, he took in the sight in front of him. Mud matted in the hair of the women. She had no gray hairs. She must have been just thirty to not have shown signs of aging. Her shirt was torn by the sleeves but remained intact. She was wearing a plaid button-down over the white shirt, contrasted with a pair of jeans. The jeans, showing signs of being battered by rain, were so dirty the color was indiscernible.

Where do I begin? The men had been shown videos of women committing cannibalism to turn. It was to harden their hatred of the witches. They began at the leg, working their way up after they had killed their target. The first step was done for him. He looked at the lady's leg. Eyeing the muck on her pants, his face soured. *Bad idea.*

The only limb he knew how to cut off without thinking was the hand. And if he was going to do this, he would need to not think. He knelt, holding his breath to keep himself from causing him to dry heave. He picked up her right hand, shivering at its coldness and shuddering at its weight. Pretending it was Analise, or any witch, he pushed his knife into the flesh below the thumb, expertly avoiding the bones.

The wrist dangled until he pulled his knife fully through. As he picked up the loose hand, he shut his eyes. Unable to keep himself from gagging, Mallor gripped the hand tighter and sobbed silent tears. He always carried a lighter, a byproduct of his training. He wasn't sure how to prepare the meat. All the videos at training had focused on the cruelty and killing done by the witches. It was forbidden to show human meat preparation after one of the original clan leaders had tried to revolt and become a wizard.

He pushed his thumb against the dial of the lighter. Then he held the hand above the flame and realized the flaw of his idea. *This would take forever. I can't look at it for much longer.*

He quickly assembled the wood for a small fire from the surrounding trees, using what foliage he could to help accelerate the fire.

He picked up the hand, spinning it over the small fire.

The smell made him gag. The only thing that kept him from hurling was he couldn't. He feared he would throw up the hand once he did try to eat it. All he could do was try. He would get back to the men, say he had eaten the deer, and move on.

An hour of slow roasting later, Mallor had not gotten any more comfortable with what he was about to do.

He had also given up on trying to be okay with it. He never would be. This was his rock bottom. The thought alone made him a bad person.

He sliced off the tops of each finger, ridding the hand of the nail. He cut above the first knuckle and below the second knuckle of the index finger. Shutting his eyes, he put the now hardened flesh into his mouth. His hands went numb immediately. Tears streamed down his face as his head hung low. *There's no turning back.*

With the chewy feeling and chicken-esque taste in his mouth, Mallor collapsed.

CHAPTER 9

———

Mallor did not wake up. He stirred and tried failingly to peel his eyes open. His limbs were paralyzed, frozen at his sides, no matter how hard his brain tried to convince them to move. Yelling at his body to respond to thoughts, Mallor's frustration caused screaming in his brain. He yelled—mentally—until his throat felt sore despite nothing having come out of it.

Move! Move! Move! Move! Move!

Having repeated the one word again and again, Mallor was exhausted. He knew cannibalism was a sin and could lead to death. He had been so desperate for food. *What an idiot! I should've just kept looking for another deer.*

He was beating himself up. Trying to reason that he had done what he thought was best at the time, his thoughts tangled into a web of self-hatred fighting with logic. He was drained, his closed eyelids growing heavier as they pressed deeper into darkness. His head began to hurt and his muscles tensed. At least he wasn't hungry.

At what cost did his full stomach come?

CHAPTER 10

What is that saying about the moment before you die?
Right, that your life flashes before your eyes.

Mallor gasped for air. His arms, reaching up, were so strained he was sure they must have rusted over at the joints. His lungs felt as though they hadn't been used in ages. His head pounded to the rhythm of his heartbeat, hands shaking as the worst migraine of his life set in. He had long since given up trying to control his limbs after his little bout with paralysis. Giving up on trying to reason out of this situation, Mallor merely wanted to feel neutral again.

And with that thought, a scream went through his body. Moving from the bottom of his diaphragm and flowing through his throat, Mallor could do nothing to stop the screech from leaving his mouth. He clutched the ground as he lay there, the noise continuing to dominate the forests. His concern ran wild, all of his training telling him to stay silent in the woods.

He began to convulse, pain soaring through his body, making him wish direly for the hurt he felt when his limbs refused to move. He wished for the pain he felt when he hid under tables and it collapsed as his father beat it through with a baseball bat trying to reach him. He yearned for the pain he felt the first night his parents gave him away, willing to trade the emotional hurt he felt thinking about how he had left his mother to rid himself of what he felt now.

The pain was scorching; red hot like the stove one touched before knowing the white surface area around the plates could heat up too. Blistering in the same way ice stuck to the tongue. It enveloped him, a high-pitched ringing destroying any chance at thought.

Opening his eyes and trying to settle the pain and ground himself, he made eye contact. Green eyes. Tan arms reached for him. A kick to the head knocked him out, and the last thing he felt was the mud under his back as he was dragged away.

———

Mallor awoke in a cell. Beyond being covered in dirt, he felt better than he ever had before. His heart still pounded, but he reveled in the bit of peace.

He shot up. *Where am I?*

He pushed himself off the cold floor of the cell, cleared his throat. "Hey! Where the hell am I? Hey! You green-eyed psycho, where are you!"

"Ugh, please shut *up.*" The female voice came from behind the door in front of him. "I am so sick of hearing you moan and groan all night. Now you choose to *scream?* Please give me a damn break."

Mallor was dumbstruck.

My body healed in the night? I shouldn't feel this good. Witch.

She was a witch. He had his doubts but didn't want to accept the defeat.

Mallor reached for his back pocket, praying his knife was there after having killed...His thought trailed off.

"What are you looking for, hunter? Your little knife? Yeah, you left that shit lodged in the wrist of that poor girl you killed."

Mallor saw red. "KILLED? I didn't *kill* anyone."

"So you're telling me you didn't eat a girl last night?"

His face grew hot, shame quickly overtaking the anger. A loud ringing began in his ears. *What had he done?*

"Oh, stop blushing, baby. We've all done it."

"So you *are* a witch?"

"Don't ask stupid questions. They told me you were smart." She rolled her eyes, condescendingly confirming his suppositions. "Of course I'm a witch."

"What did you do to me? Why don't I hurt anymore?"

"Baby, I didn't do anything to you. You did this yourself."

"What?"

She had come out from behind the door and was looking him up and down, her green eyes bringing back the memory of every time he had been kicked in the head. She took a breath in as if exasperated by Mallor's stupidity. She turned around, walking away.

Under her breath she muttered, "Remember what Ana told you, Lina. Remember not to kill the boy. He is, after all, our only wizard."

Could it be true? Tipping back into the wall, Mallor reached for anything to steady him. Gravity quickly got the best of him, and he fell to the hard cinderblock floor beneath him. Staring into space, his thoughts ran wild. Unable to answer his own questions, he did what he was apparently now best at.

His scream quickly developed into a sob calling for help. His training had prepared him for a lot, but never for this level of pain. *Teil, where are you? Please come save me.* Begging to a God he had never believed in, he sobbed for his lost friend and his lost life. His head began to pound harder, the tears streaming into his mouth as if he were a five-year-old after a tantrum.

Head in his hands, Mallor jumped when Lina hit the poles of the cell, making a loud ring on the metal. He sniffled and tried to wipe his tears away.

"What the hell are you crying for?"

"I wasn't crying." His sniffles made him wildly unconvincing.

"Okay, big boy." Lina, clearly not the type to ask a question twice especially when it was out of consolation, began to walk away. The bat in her hand scraped across the poles causing Mallor's head to throb.

"No. Stop."

"I don't take orders from prisoners, sweetheart."

Mallor sunk back into the corner. Witches were brutal, and while his ego fueled heavy backtalk on most days, he was hopeless.

Lina rolled her eyes. "Ugh, what do you want, then? Ready to tell me why you're crying?"

"What do you mean, *why am I crying*?"

He was shocked at her idiocy. She had just mumbled he was a wizard and walked away! Why else would he be pissed off?

Lina shrugged as if she had never had an original thought in the world.

Mallor was ready to rip her head off. "Are you *an idiot*?" He launched himself against the cell door, gripping the bars as he screamed at her.

She didn't even flinch. "Chill, wizard-boy. I don't waste time trying to figure out why people are piss babies."

Mallor hadn't had to practice this kind of self-control in ages. Taking a deep but very shaky breath in, he settled. Loosening his grip of the bars, feeling smaller than he ever had before, he asked the question that would break him.

"Am I a wizard?"

"Oh, *that's* what you've been panicking about? No, no you're not a wizard." Lina began to chuckle.

Mallor, unable to control his joy, laughed, the biggest smile spreading on his mouth.

"Oh, shit. You *believed* that? No, yeah, you're definitely a wizard."

Mallor went through all the feelings of shock one more time. However, this time, he was void of anger.

"Are you just going to...stand still? Oh, oh, you're in shock. Okay, enjoy that!" Lina began to walk away.

"Wait! Come back. Please."

Lina turned around and groaned. "You're lucky Ana doesn't need me right now. Go on."

Mallor took in a deep breath, relaxing his shoulders from the tense position they had been in for ages.

Where do I start?

"How did this happen?"

"I'm not sure, really. Ana had been saying your name from the beginning." Lina's response only aggravated him, her casual demeanor feeling inappropriate for the fact his life was changing.

"Who's Ana?" Mallor furrowed his brow, confused by a name he had never heard and angered by the possibility this "Ana" could be the reason for his misfortune.

"She said you knew her. Analise? From Cinder?" Lina had started chewing gum, her voice ringing with absolute boredom.

Mallor, on the other hand, did not find any of this boring.

Ana had done this to him. He would have to process his anger later, because for the time being this could mean he was close to Teil.

"Okay, so we're in Cinder then. That's good to know."

"Oh, we're not in Cinder. Didn't you hear? Ana split from the family months ago."

"Isn't the Election soon? Why would she split?"

"No one knows. She was just adamant we leave. I used to be her servant."

Mallor knew why she left. She must have left because of the abuse. While his heart twinged for her, he was too distressed to dwell on it. He needed to get his questions out.

"What did she want with me?"

"To turn you, of course! Don't waste my time with stupid questions." Lina checked her watch, as if her mention of time reminded her she had places to be. "I have to go. Ana will be convening the coven heads soon."

"What? No, please! I have more questions! How am I a wizard?" Mallor's words came out in a slur. "Please, take me to Analise."

"She hates being called Analise."

"Take me to her. Please." Mallor hoped the desperation in his voice would persuade her.

She didn't flinch. "I can't. The tests are soon."

With those words, Lina waved her hand and a sharp pain splintered through his arms.

"What are you do—"

His body growing light, eyelids heavy, Mallor fainted.

When he awoke, he was no longer on the floor of the cell. Rather comfy, his eyes slowly opened, his vision blurred as if he needed glasses. He had always prided himself on his perfect eyesight, he didn't have to worry about breaking a pair during a fight.

He was numb, although conscious again. His shoulder should have been sore from falling backward onto the cinderblock floor earlier but it wasn't, although a bright blue bruise had formed. His arms were strapped to the sides of the medical gurney. Struggling, he grunted as he tried to pull himself free, but the cuffs seared him.

They must have been charmed. Struggling would only hurt him.

"Hey! Is anyone there? Come out, coward!" His throat hurt, but determination coursed through his body with each scream. "Show me who you are! You'll be damned before I let you—"

"Oh, please be quiet." A woman with long, dark hair, likely in her mid-thirties appeared above him. "Lina was right, you really never shut up."

"*Answer me.*"

He'd had enough of being held captive by these disgusting witches.

"I can't hear you, love." The woman sneered. Mallor realized he must have been silenced with a charm, or behind some forcefield he couldn't see. "We have things to do, and your screams are only inconvenient." She seemed smug, satisfied with herself for having thought of ways to torture him beyond the physical.

Mallor hated her. She was the reason all witches were horrible. They were cruel, unforgiving, and selfish. He stuck his tongue out at her.

Her laughs dominated the room. Doubling over, she was louder than the machine that lay beeping by his head. His face began to heat up out of embarrassment and frustration.

His actions were childish, but he hadn't felt this angry in a long time. He coped with anger through cruel words and killing witches. Right now, he couldn't do neither.

"This will be a lot easier if you just let it happen," she said.

Mallor mouthed a very cruel sentence, making it clear she could screw herself. Topping it off, he whispered, "Over my dead body."

"When will you get it through your head *I can't hear you?*" She smiled a sickly-sweet smile. "And, even if I could, you wouldn't get a word in edgewise."

Was she intending on talking the whole time? The only thing worse than being tortured to near death through tests was being spoken to by a *witch* the whole time.

His worst fears came true as she took her syringe filled with blue liquid and shoved it into the vein below his elbow on his forearm.

"So how do you feel about abandoning your clan? From what we hear, you're the big man on campus. Big, giant pain in the ass for the rest of us, you hunters. How do you think they'll feel when they hear you're *one of us?* Have you ever heard the saying about how you don't treat your friends poorly?

Was she implying she would treat him well? Because the electrical shock went through his body as she continued to poke at every juicy vein of his stated otherwise.

"Sweetheart, you may have committed cannibalism, but you will *never* be like us. This pain you're feeling, this is the *easiest* it will ever get."

He should have known. He had no people anymore. He could never return to his clan. He winced, both from the blood that began dripping from his forehead into his eye and from the aching pain in his heart. He was alone once again, like the little boy who hid under the dining table from pain.

His vision was still blurred, so all he could see were the movements of her arms and her smile as she chatted away, saying statements that would pour salt into his wounds and random gossip. He learned her name was Lily. He couldn't help but snicker to himself, knowing Lily could never come from Lillian but only from Lilith. He was sure he was in front of a demon. Then again, when faced with a witch, he always felt he was in the face of a demon.

And now he was one of them.

She had shaved his head, he realized, then she pushed a syringe into his chest.

A tear fell from his eye, mixing with the blood still dripping. All the physical pain was gone, eaten by the hurt for the life he had lost forever.

He suspected a few days had passed as the Lily—or Lilith, as he had begun calling her in his head—left and returned more than twice. The room, clearly in the basement of a building, had no windows. Mallor hadn't seen the sun in ages, and he was dying to move. While his vision was still blurry, even the distant pictures of his clan marching kept him alive. And, it was a real fight to stay alive. His body was pushing back against everything Lilith put in him.

He winced, recalling the time she'd placed a cloth on his forearm. Thinking it was to cool down the skin that had bruised from being punctured again and again, he grew hopeful. The purple washcloth touched his skin and immediately began to burn. He had writhed in pain, too proud to beg her to stop but too weak to keep his body from showing her how much he needed her to stop. She giggled, pressing the cloth in further.

He was sure he would have at least a second-degree burn, and quickly realized the only way to get past this was to grow detached. He lowered his shoulders from his ears, stopped clutching his jaw and core. He shut his eyes, willing this to end.

Losing himself in thought, he began to hatch a plan. While he knew there was a chance, he wouldn't come out of these tests alive, he hoped Analise had turned him for a purpose. *Turned him.* He was disgusted. He deserved the pain Lilith was inflicting upon him. He only wished it was a hunter doing it, earning the glory of having killed a witch. It was the least he could do after the atrocity he had committed.

He could lie.

There were a few days until the Election, if Mallor was guesstimating time correctly. He could return to his men, and never show he was a wizard. Quite frankly, he didn't even *know* if he was a wizard. He hadn't shown any bout of power, unsure what he could do. They were never shown spells in training, at least never shown how they were done.

He lay here feeling helpless, knowing he was theoretically the most powerful man in the world. He had already tried to force out a spell, do something. But with his hands tied down and Lilith in front of him, he had no mobility to practice a spell even if Lilith hadn't restricted his magic through a charm.

Mallor needed his people back. He would give up all the power in the world to be back with Tate and the Court, even Cell! He wanted so badly to listen to them drone on and on about strategy as they fought. Fighting was the only thing that ever made sense to him. He didn't even know if he could fight his way out of here.

He would need magic. It was the only way he could face what seemed like a village of witches. Especially if they were trained by Analise, he wouldn't make it out alive.

She could train him! Analise must have needed him for something. Why else would he be here? If he could just convince her magical training was appropriate for her goal, he could learn how to use his training against her. In three days? Four if he were lucky? He wasn't sure how he would make it work. All he knew was he was a fast learner and he would need to get out of here.

But first, he had to get rid of Lilith. Pulling a page out of a children's movie, he decided to play dead.

Lilith barely noticed his stillness at first.

He would be lying if he said playing dead while being tortured by medical instruments was helpful. He found solace in taking deep breaths when she turned around to scribble notes in her notebook. He lay still, hoping and praying she would begin to panic and take him out of the room. He didn't know how to find Analise, but he knew they would want to save him. Whoever "they" were.

Lilith screamed. "Mallor, you idiot. Wake up." There was true fear in her voice, as if she was running from someone. "Ana told me to test your limits. You are *not* allowed to die." Her voice grew shakier with a sense of urgency.

She grabbed his shoulders and shook him.

Mallor kept his eyes shut.

"You are *not* allowed to die. Do you hear me? Mallor, she'll kill me if you do."

At that moment, he almost wished he was dead. That way, Lilith would go too. She deserved nothing but the worst.

No, he would lay still.

"Ugh! This is why hunters are the worst. Damn near anything kills you."

She continued to curse but wheeled him out of the room. Hearing the doors open, he silently whispered, "Yes!" He couldn't have been more thrilled. The easiest trick in the book might work!

CHAPTER 11

———

Mallor's eyes fluttered awake, taking in the sunlight that peered through the billowy, white blinds in front of him. The sun warmed his skin, and a smile crept up as the sides of his lips turned up in joy. He took in the second of silence and sunshine that complimented his well-rested feeling.

"So Cell, what's the pla—" He propped himself up on his elbow, looking to speak with Cell about the day. As he did, however, his heart fell into his chest. His smile faded, and he rolled back over to shut his eyes for a bit longer, yearning for the peace he had felt just a second ago.

"Who's Cell?" a soft voice spoke, coated in warmth and words dripping like gold.

He turned over, not sure what to expect, but made contact with a soft, green set of eyes with full lashes.

Analise.

Her hair was the same dirty blonde, spilling down her back and shoulders. She sat in a wooden chair; chin held high with the posture of a leader. The very sun that greeted Mallor coated her in gold, giving shadows to every contour of her décolletage while revealing glowing shoulders.

Where had the little girl running for bags of blood gone?

"Did you hear me? Who's Cell?"

He stopped staring, remembering who she had taken him from.

"A good friend. Someone I'll never know again thanks to you."

She rolled her eyes, leaving Mallor with irritation. "Don't act like you're sad you're now the most powerful man in the world." She ran her fingers through her hair, looping it into a low ponytail. "I've done you a favor."

He was having a hard time keeping his composure. He needed to sit up if he was going to sound like the intelligent hunter he was. Right now, laying on his side, he looked helpless. More than that, he felt small and wildly human next to Analise.

I'm no longer human. The thought angered him, causing him to sit up and tense.

"A *favor*? You've turned me into the thing I hate the most."

"Please! Don't pin this on me. You took the chance to eat that poor girl. That was *your* choice."

"How did you know about that?"

"Well, I put her there, of course! Who do you think the deer was?"

"What do you mean *who?*"

"Lily, of course! Couldn't you tell by her eyes?"

Was she insinuating he was stupid? Or worse, unobservant?

"You mean *Lilith?*" He smirked at his nickname for her. "See, that would have been possible if she hadn't been trying to kill me during our lovely time together. How the hell is that even possible anyway?" He had heard of witches with crazy powers, but shapeshifting was not one of them.

"Why don't you tell me how you're feeling fine now when Lily brought you in nearly dead? Your pulse had just about disappeared."

Mallor was shocked his body had eased so quickly. Maybe it was a witch thing he could do now?

"And, how did you know Lily's full name? She never tells anyone."

He chuckled. "Wait, that's *really* her name? She's really named after an ancient Sumerian demon?"

"Not named after. She *is* Lilith. It's why she can shapeshift."

How little he knew about what existed. Having a Sumerian demon on your side would change the entire outcome of any fight. There was not a single hunter who knew Lilith existed. Suddenly, his nickname for her wasn't so comedic.

"Don't look so surprised. When are you going to realize how much there is you don't know?" She sighed. "You hunters are all the same. So distracted by your prejudices you miss knowledge that could actually help you win your fight." Analise stood up, pushing her chair back under the desk, which Mallor assumed was the nurse's.

"Where are you going? I have more questions." Remembering how weak he needed to sound to make his fake death scare seem believable, he quickly tacked on, "And I'm still exhausted. Stay here."

"Oh, I knew you weren't dead. The dead don't breathe."

She looked at him, puzzled by his request. "You want me to...stay?"

"Um, yes. I still don't know what's going on."

Her shoulders tensed up, rising closer to her ears. For a second, just one, her guard had come down. But that was gone now. Mallor was unsure why she suddenly seemed cold again, but the change in mood was so subtle he chose to overlook it. He had bigger fish to fry than why a seventeen-year-old girl was moody.

"I have things to do," she said. "I'll have the nurse bring you to my office at lunch. You can ask me your questions then."

"Will you give me answers?"

"See you in a bit, Mallor. Oh, and have the nurse give you something more...*presentable*."

He looked down and blushed at the white paper gown. A blanket covered his bottom half, but he was nearly naked. He looked up, hoping to apologize, but before he could, the big, wooden door slammed shut.

CHAPTER 12

His solemn goodbye to the sun in the hospital room was purposeless, although he had fallen in love with it. The second the wooden doors shut behind Mallor, he was greeted with a blinding hallway made of glass windows. Each protected by dark-green curtains, he appreciated the curtains were tucked off to the side revealing the outside world.

Smiling, he walked behind Analise, taking in the scene. Behind the windows were acres upon acres of greenery. The fall leaves coated some of the grass, but much of it still looked as beautiful as it would in late spring. There was no one outside. It looked nearly desolate, but from meeting the nurse and Lilith, it was clear there were people here.

"Is this a different part of Cinder? It doesn't look like anything I saw last time I was here."

She winced. "No, we are no longer in Cinder."

"Where are we then?"

"I would prefer it if you held off on your questions until we reach my office."

She hadn't turned around once to look at him as she spoke. She merely trusted he was following her. Okay, maybe it wasn't trust, but entitlement. It didn't look like anyone here defied her, not even Lilith. When a real demon doesn't argue with you, the respect was earned.

He wasn't sure how she had earned this, but he did know she had answers. He continued walking forward.

At the end of the hall, a short staircase led them into a new corridor. Here, the natural light disappeared, leaving the space to its own dark guises. Walls were coated in deep-maroon paint and little gargoyles sat between each door in a little nook in the wall.

"Woah." Mallor couldn't keep the word to himself. Paintings swallowed the ceiling, leaving no blank space to be found. The paintings were of women undergoing the transformation, starting with the killing of a human. While wildly mortifying and making his stomach churn, he couldn't help but admire the art. The faces were hyper realistic, and all of the clothes shone as if they were made out of oil paints that would never dry.

Analise turned around, her hair falling out if its loose ponytail, "The paintings are beautiful, aren't they? The nurse does them between tending to patients." There was a smile in her voice when discussing the nurse, and he assumed the nurse must be equally maternal to everyone. She bent over to pick up her hair tie.

They continued to walk on hardwood floors the same dark brown as the large doors from the infirmary. Each of the doors they passed had a little drawing on the front, as if this were summer camp and students were pasting name tags. Every door was shut, which only increased his curiosity.

As they walked further, they finally came to a dark-purple door so rich in color it was nearly black, and it swung open on command from a swish of her hand.

"Well, what are you waiting for?"

Mallor set foot in the room, taking in the scent of wood and old paper. Two stories tall, books took up every bit of the walls. Ladders upon ladders were set up to help reach them, and in the center was a single desk. Expansive, the mahogany desk was the centerpiece of the room. On it were trinkets, few of which Mallor recognized. Relieved by the familiarity of a stapler, he watched as Analise sat in a large, purple chair behind the desk. The chair, closer to lavender, brought out the lighter streaks of blonde in her hair.

"Are you going to stare all day or ask me some questions? I don't have time to waste."

"Right." He wasn't sure where to start beyond sitting up straight. "How did this happen?"

"You ate someone. That's how this happened."

He couldn't help but wince at the blunt acknowledgment of what he had done. He was too exhausted and in too much pain to feel the full extent of his shame. Regardless, it sat like a stone in the pit of his stomach. He had betrayed everything he had ever stood for.

Pushing it to the side every time it came to the forefront of his mind, he tried to justify his decision with the fact he'd done it for the right cause. He was still determined to destroy the witches, and he knew he could hide his secret. He may even be able to use it to his advantage.

"Don't give me a useless answer," he said.

"I'm happy to stop giving you answers at all, Mallor." She was cold, but he could hear a smile in her voice.

"I'm not really sure you've got the right to be giving me an attitude, Analise. You've ruined my life, here."

The room was suffocating, and the rhythm of the argument distressed him. It was like the first time they had met all over again.

Analise rolled her eyes and scoffed. "Lily told me you were whining about this. I didn't ruin your life, Mallor. This is a reward."

Any type of banter had disappeared. Mallor grew stone cold.

"Reward for what? You've turned me into everything I hate. You've made me like *you*." A sour taste was growing in his mouth and his stomach began to turn.

"Like me? You *wish* you had my power. I remember when we first met, you were sitting there in fear of me. No one has ever feared you like that."

He had no words. How could this lunatic of a woman ever believe he wanted to be like her? He also had no rebuttal to the fact no one had feared him the way they feared her. She was truly mortifying, despite the fact he'd never let himself admit it.

Mallor sat there, arms crossed and back stiff. He clenched his jaw, knowing it would be sore later.

"Why me?"

He didn't know how else to express his displeasure for this unfortunate twist of events. He was praying it was a game of chance, but he could see in her eyes she had done this to him for a reason. Was it revenge? All he had done was help her and open his heart to her.

He immediately regretted his empathy toward her that day. He had lost Teil to a moment of weakness and now had lost his way of life.

Her answer had better be perfect.

"Here, have some tea." Analise pushed her chair back and stood up. Heading to a glass cart under an abstract painting Mallor couldn't be bothered with, she began to pour from a white kettle. The kettle, adorned in butterflies, matched the teacups she set out. There was a little clink so faint it could only be heard due to the silence stewing between them.

"I don't want any goddamn tea, Ana." Mallor couldn't help but feel the lie in his words. He was dehydrated and worn out. Tea was always what he and his mother drank to help him settle after a rough encounter with his father, and Ana made him chamomile just like she had.

"Don't lie to yourself." Her tone was caring, despite being coated in ice. "Drink the tea, Mallor. Your questions are a waste of my time, so I figure I'll just explain what I can."

Showing a bit of truce without having to thank her, he reluctantly reached for the teacup. Lacing his finger through the handle, the warmth of the glass soothed him.

"This wasn't unintentional. We chose you." She paused, letting him take in the information. "When we first met, I was impressed by your strategy even though I knew what you were planning. Hoping to bring my sisters together and kill us all? It was so transparent."

Mallor was reeling too much to feel the impact of her backhanded compliment.

"It was clear you were young but showed promise. I later peeked through my mother's files as Teil mentioned you when locked in his cell. He begged to know if you were okay. It was quite irritating, really."

"Teil?" It took everything in his power to spit the name out. He was outraged by the disrespect of him, but eager to know if Teil was still alive.

She waved her hand, dismissing the question. "We can talk about him later. Let's stay on track. I've got things to do and while you're an asset to me, I can't sit around with you all day as you look like an idiot with a baffled look on your face." She sipped her tea. "I want you to take down Cinder with me. And not just them for that matter, but all eight covens."

"Aren't we in Cinder?"

"I thought you were observant and a good listener. Does it *look* like we're in Cinder? I already told you we weren't." Her patience was wearing thin.

"How would I know? You've kept me locked up and tortured me!"

"Lily tortured you. I don't take part in abuse without cause. You know that."

"You sure as hell endorsed it!" A low blow, but it was true.

"There are things I have to do here to keep the peace. I run this place. We aren't in Cinder. I took my closest allies, those who had seen my sister's abuse firsthand, and created my own coven."

Mallor was in disbelief at her idiocy. "Creating a coven? Who do you think you are? No one has that power. Just because the Original Witch has passed away gives you no right to play god. We don't need more witches, anyway. *The Red Book* forbids dissenters from the original eight and you *know* that."

"*The Red Book* is outdated. It's led to abuse between families and rivalries that shouldn't exist. The witches don't need to be enemies to humans, yet it's all they've promoted."

"Yes, because you *eat people.*"

"Not just me, Mallor. You do, too."

"I *did.* Past tense. I wanted to survive."

"Don't we all want to survive? Many women do it for different reasons! The years of sexism and patriarchy that ruled our lives stripped us from any power in human society."

"Oh, please. It's just a claim to power."

"You're telling me if men had the ability to become wizards, they wouldn't?"

Mallor had no answer to this question. He had seen what the light of power had done to the men he trained. For many of them, it was what pushed them to be better. It was often what pushed *him* to be better.

"Your silence really is deafening." She sipped from her cup, nudging with her head to push him to sip from his. Not knowing his glass was empty, he tipped it to show her. As she chuckled, she poured him another. "Good to know tea is the way to your heart."

Mallor smirked, finding himself somewhat still at ease despite whatever crazy nonsense was coming out of her mouth. "I will say, stalling with tea isn't the smartest strategy."

"Seems to be working so far." She sent a smug smile his way. "Besides, at this rate you'll have to use the restroom. That's what I call a stall."

"Poor strategy is revealing your plan." Mallor cupped the tea and smiled at the warmth.

"Like I was saying, I want to eliminate the original eight. If our power is strong enough—"

"Let me just stop you right there. There is no, *our* power. There is you, a witch, and me, a hunter. You are my sworn enemy and that doesn't magically change because you've tricked me into a mistake."

"You really are a hunter. Blaming everyone else for your own mistakes. It's just like the polarization between witches and the world. It was created by your kind telling others we were a threat."

"You *are* a threat! You eat people."

In proper Analise fashion, she waved her one good hand to push the topic to the side, a small scar sitting where he had originally cut into it.

"Can we stay on topic for one minute, please? You're wasting my time."

They locked eyes. A second passed and Mallor spoke and broke the moment. "Fine."

"We want to train you. Make you our secret weapon. My magic has been running low since the...brief injury of my hand." Mallor shuffled awkwardly as she seemed hesitant to talk about the injury he had inflicted upon her. "If we train you, we can bring you to the Election to destroy the others. That is, of course, if you take to the training well."

Just a sliver of hope. All he had to do was train to get back to his men. He could do this. This was, in fact, truly the only thing he knew how to do. He would have to find a way to sneak away once there. He could even kill the original eight and Analise if he played his cards right.

"Okay."

"That's it? You don't have any other questions?" Analise looked puzzled, furrowing her brow in confusion.

"Are you trying to make this harder for yourself?"

"No that's not what I—"

"Listen." He would have to lie through his teeth to make this work. "All I know how to do is fight." This part was easy; he wasn't lying just yet. "But I believe the world would be better—safer—if the witches got along. And you're right. *The Red Book* is outdated. None of the rules make much sense, and the tension between the covens is dangerous for everyone."

Mallor mentally patted himself on the back. The world could never have peace if the witches existed. He was born to get rid of them, and if playing Analise was what it took, he could do it.

When he was younger, his dad would tell him to make choices "for the greater good." When he got older, he knew his dad was playing him and using it to excuse abuse. But now, he wondered if he understood in a new context.

"Fair enough." She still sounded suspicious, but it was clear she wasn't going to question him going along with her plan.

What choice did she have anyway? The Election was just three days away and he would need to gain control over his abilities fast if she were going to take him.

Mallor stood up, taking Analise's cup and setting it back on the tray to clean up. He felt her eyes linger on him as he moved across the room, feeling her gaze linger.

All the dishes stacked, and tea returned to its original place, he said, "So should we get started?" His voice was cocky, and although he was worn out, he was thrilled to fight. And although he didn't want to admit it, he wondered about his powers.

"Not so fast. How about you take a shower?" She laughed, bringing his excitement down a peg.

A shower did sound fantastic.

"I'll show you to your room," she said, "and have Lily bring you to the training chamber in an hour."

"Hell no, keep that psycho demon away from me." His stomach turned at the thought of seeing Lilith again.

"You might be important, but you don't make those decisions around here. Get used to Lily. And never call her Lilith unless you want to die." She stood up, smoothing out her clothing. "Come on now."

Weaving through the halls again, Mallor was shocked by the sheer size of the estate Analise had built. They walked in silence, her shoes clicking every time she stepped forward on the hardwood floor. The entire building was colored dark, but bits of natural light streamed in, warming his face. He was thankful for the silence, but he wasn't able to use it for strategy drafting. He figured he'd shower and try to nap for forty minutes, or at least until Lilith inevitably ruined his day when she came to get him.

Analise came to an abrupt stop. Crashing into her, he blushed, mumbling an apology under his breath for looking at his shoes as he walked.

She rolled her eyes and gave him instructions. "This is where you'll be staying during your time here. And if you prove to be an asset to the team, you can stay here permanently. I assume it's been a long time since you've had your own room, or at least, that's what they told us in school."

"Yes." There was no point in denying the fact his entire young adult life had been spent sleeping in a room nearly stacked to the brim with men. He also knew better than to reveal any other details. Besides, who knew what the witches were told in school? He wasn't going to give her any more information than she may have already had. "Is there a key?"

"A key? No." She waved her hand over the doorknob, and a small click led to the door flying open and hitting the wall behind it.

Having only ever seen magic used to harm hunters, he was blown away by the simple task performed in front of him. He also felt just a bit helpless he didn't know how to do it himself. Was he going to have to relearn everything about life? He felt like an infant.

"How do I do that? Are you going to have to walk me to my room every time?"

"You wish."

The flirty nature of Analise's comment took him aback. "Teach me."

She shut the door manually, then reached for his right hand, and held it. "This is your dominant hand, right?"

Mallor nodded, his exhaustion and desire to learn mixing with his deep confusion.

"Just think about the outcome," she said. "Find the spot in your brain right above where your thoughts and emotions are, and as you see the door unlock, just wave your hand over the knob."

He shut his eyes, focusing on what she said.

"Do it with your eyes open. Many of our younger witches start with their eyes closed for visualization, but with how little time we have, you'll have to get good at this now."

He blinked, softening his gaze. He pictured the gold knob, the inside workings of the door cooperating with him to get him to the shower and away from the witches. Then, as if the click of the lock in his head translated into real life, he unsoftened his gaze and the door creaked open. While it didn't fly open, he had performed his first spell. He felt...*powerful*. He didn't like it. Or maybe he didn't like that he did like it.

Analise smiled, putting her arm out gesturing at him to enter the room. She stood just in the doorway laughing at his shock. "Take your time to take this all in. Well, maybe not too long. Lilith will be here in an hour."

Before he could respond, the door shut with a whoosh and Analise was gone.

He was alone, but he almost—*almost*—missed her.

CHAPTER 13

———

Mallor forgot about Analise's quick exit as soon as he turned away from the door. His jaw dropped. A bedroom adorned with high ceilings swallowed him, and he took in the deep-maroon furniture by a beige wall. A four-poster bed caught his eye, larger than anything he had ever slept in. Bits of gold lined the moldings in the room and further complimented the details adorning the beautiful etches in the dark wood. There was a desk, equipped with notebooks and a fountain pen that looked more expensive than anything he had ever owned.

Touching the bed sheets, the satin felt like heaven between his fingers. On the far side of the room was a large window covering nearly the entire wall, and in front of that a small couch. Mallor smiled at the books upon books creating a reading space.

No aspect of the bedroom compared to the bathroom. An automated door right after the bedroom entrance opened, revealing marble floor and black, wood counters. A bath stood next to a massive rain shower, causing him to go nearly into shock as he set foot into the space.

The floors were warm, clearly heated for comfort. He didn't even bother locking the door; he merely stripped, tossing his clothing into an opening in the wall labeled "laundry chute." He had never seen such a thing, but he assumed the laundry ended up somewhere where it would be washed.

Twisting the silver shower dial, he waited for the water to steam up the room. He was astonished this kind of wealth existed, having tossed the idea of ever living this lavishly to the side. Thinking about a lifestyle like this had only ever upset him, and now it was his. Well, for now.

The thought of this being temporary snapped him back into reality. He slid the shower door open and poured soap into his hands. He quickly scrubbed shampoo into his hair, trying not to dwell on how little of it was now left after Lilith shaved it. The shampoo smelled like eucalyptus, and it took everything in his power not to melt into the relaxing scent instead of planning out what his next steps would be.

So long as he excelled in training—which he knew he would—he would be able to get to the Election. The difficult part would be finding a way to reunite with his men once he was there. He would need Analise to trust him if he were going to find a way to kill her once there.

It was then he realized what he could offer her that no witch could have: love.

Mallor would pretend to fall for her, giving her a taste of companionship. He didn't know very much about dating, given his limited experience as a teenage boy with parents who hated one another. Flirting was foreign to him, but some part of this had to be natural. Right?

He continued to lather his body with soap, eventually throwing a liquid labeled "conditioner" in his hair. While the shower pressure and warm water relaxed his muscles, the water was stinging the cuts on his body, forcing him to remember Lilith would be back soon. He wanted to rest, determined to take a nap no matter how much it discombobulated him when he awoke. *He would need his bearings if he were to train to be a wizard and make his trainer fall in love with him in three days.*

Replaying that sentence in his head, he realized just how odd his life was.

He turned the shower off with a creak, wrapping a white towel around his waist. Smiling at the warmth of the towel, he took a second to breathe and enjoy the peace. He opened the closet next to his bed, shock consuming him yet again at the sheer abundance of his environment.

It looked like Analise had provided him with every article of clothing he could have possibly wanted. He didn't have the energy to process more shock, so he merely fell asleep naked, embracing the soft satin sheets. He may not have known how to flirt or do magic, but he sure as hell knew how to sleep.

If felt as though less than five minutes had passed before he heard a stern knock on the door.

"Get your ass up, wizard!"

Despite his frustration with having been woken up so abrasively, he heard the upbeat voice and sighed with relief, knowing it wasn't Lilith. He was also thankful this place—wherever he was—taught people the manners of knocking.

"Coming!" he said and snatched a pair of black training sweats and a short sleeve sweat-wicking shirt from the closet. He was surprised at how well everything fit, even the boxers, but knew he needed to get a move on.

The knock came again.

"Let's go!"

He swung the door open to reveal Lina. While she was equally frustrating, he was thrilled to see her over his torturer.

"Hey."

He was surprised by how calm he sounded, but he couldn't help but know her goofy attitude put him at ease. He was going to have to let bygones be bygones if he were to survive working with these people.

"You know what? The buzz cut looks good."

Mallor rolled his eyes at Lina's comment, but couldn't help it when the sides of his mouth moved into a smile reacting to the small boost of confidence.

"So how was the room?" Lina walked in front of him but turned around to address him as she spoke. "Ana really went all out for you." She turned back around continuing to walk, turning the corners the same way they came.

"It's beautiful. Truly. The shower is great, too."

"Ah, see, I knew you smelled better!" She laughed at her joke, garnering a quiet chuckle out of him.

A short silence followed, but Mallor quickly realized Lina's talkative nature would rarely keep her quiet. In fact, it was a miracle she had tried to withhold information the first time they met.

They weaved through the corridors as she continued to ask him questions. She was intrigued by the life of a hunter, wanting to know how one could survive so long on so little.

"It's not that I am used to extravagance, per se. But I do understand the value of fresh clothes every morning and meals that actually respond to habitual hunger cues."

Mallor couldn't help but smile as a witch told him she wasn't used to luxury. Her alluring nature, combined with her classy-yet-battle-based wardrobe, juxtaposed by the paintings on the ceilings and long, dark curtains was the textbook definition of lavish. While she didn't carry herself nearly as gracefully as Analise did, she surely kept a bit of class with her despite her love for rambling.

While she pelted him with questions about hunting and the clan system, Mallor had to remember to hold his tongue to not reveal too much information. He was thrilled to be talking about the thing he was best at, but it could all be used against the men he had trained.

There were secrets the witches didn't know, and most of the time, those secrets were the only thing keeping them alive. Hunters were never one step ahead of the witches; that was damn near impossible. They were, however, usually in step with them.

The clans were well trained in anticipating where the witches were and where they were coming from. Word of mouth spread most of their information, but great war strategists like Cell were able to predict the decisions of the witches after many years of practice. Cell was significantly older than Mallor, but that was normal and expected due to the integral nature of the job. If Cell failed, they all did.

Lina made Mallor smile, and it brought out the joy in his voice recounting adventures, although he fibbed about certain parts.

"So tell me about Teil. He was a hunter of yours, right?" Lina's statement came out casually and was clearly well-intentioned.

Mallor's heart fell into his stomach, and he found his foot getting caught on the carpet, catching himself before he tripped over nothing.

She turned around, stopping and putting her arm out in case she had to catch him.

"Sorry," he said. "I'm fine. Just haven't heard that name in a while."

A lie. All he had thought about for the past few days since Leon's was Teil. He wanted to know if he was alive, and he thought about what a hero he would be if he reunited with his men and brought Teil with him. He had to play his cards right. If he was going to get Teil back, he couldn't make him look like something of importance. If he did, he was sure Analise would use Teil as leverage over him.

"He wasn't a hunter of mine. I was younger at the time, making Teil a trainer."

"A trainer, or *your* trainer?"

Lina knew something. A question like that was pushy, especially because he hadn't specified any of those details. Most people would assume Teil was not Mallor's trainer.

"No, not mine. I didn't really know him, honestly. I just heard he was a nice guy."

"Was?"

"Yeah. He passed away on a Cinder mission a few years ago. I was with him."

"Oh, right! That's how you know Ana." She avoided confirming or denying Teil's death.

Mallor figured it was best they switched topics before he really figured out what his plan for finding Teil would be. He would just have to stay hopeful, relying on Leon's knowledge Teil was, in fact, alive.

"Do you guys have trainers?" he asked her.

"Hold that thought. We've come to the training room." Lina pushed open two large black doors, looking as if they led into a vault. "I'll be escorting you around for the most part, so you'll have plenty of time to ask questions."

Mallor was surprised Lilith wasn't the one doing this job. Had Analise noticed how uncomfortable Lilith made him, or was it just a coincidence? He didn't have time to figure it out now as Lina shoved him through the doors, waved goodbye. The vault shut with a thud, the loud noise coinciding with lights flickering on.

"I see you showered! Great news." Analise's voice came from the far end of the room as she walked her way over to him. She had changed, now wearing a black training suit and combat boots.

"Put this in your dominant hand." She handed him a stick of metal in the shape of a wand.

"What is this?" Mallor had never been told witches had wands. That was always a myth from the fantasy books that had existed before witches were real. Every clip Mallor had seen or any encounter he had with a witch led them to use their hands. "It looks like a wand?"

"It *is* a wand, stupid." She rolled her eyes in disbelief. "If you're going to keep asking wasteful questions like this, training you is going to get really old really fast."

"I just didn't realize you used them." Mallor realized he had given away a gap in the hunters' knowledge. He kicked himself, reminding himself to be more tactful over these next two days. Otherwise, he would never make it back to his old life.

"Hold the wand firmly. Every young witch learns magic using a wand. Typically, it takes them a few months before being able to feel the magic in their fingertips. However, given you are a hunter and know how to channel your emotions to reach a goal, we're hoping you'll be ready in three days. On the third day, we'll teleport early in the morning to the Election site."

"Teleport?"

Without hesitation, Analise shoved away his concern. "It's easy. You'll learn how to do it the morning of. Not that I don't trust you, but I'd rather you not disappear on me."

"Okay. Where do we begin?"

CHAPTER 14

"We'll just start with a few warm-up spells. Magic is largely nonverbal. You might use words to express your anger, but you have to root into a negative emotion to channel power."

"Negative? Why not something like happiness?"

"When you commit cannibalism, it is the negative experiences of the person you have eaten that lets you access magic. You do not absorb their joy."

"Well, that's grim." Mallor's face soured as if he had just licked a lemon.

"It's actually rather interesting. Soon enough, you'll be able to harness the exact negative memories of the person you've eaten. You'll be able to see their memories and pick the ones that hurt the most, increasing your power."

Mallor was growing queasy at the idea of physically using someone's worst memories to make himself better at magic. "For now, however, the power you have through your own bad memories should suffice. And if Lily told me correctly, you seem to have a lot of bad memories."

"How would Lilith know that?" He was tapping his foot, growing anxious at what she knew. "She was too busy torturing me to have asked me anything."

"She was torturing you so she wouldn't have to ask you, silly." Analise began setting up targets and sounded so at ease despite what she had revealed. She and Lilith knew his worst memories.

"How?"

"What do you think all the poking and probing was for?" Mallor grew silent.

Analise was too busy setting up to look at him but realized a bit too late now he was scared beyond belief. "Stop worrying!" She put the last target on the wall and walked back toward him. "We all go through this. You only have to be probed once, and it is never painful."

"I promise you it was painful."

"Well, Lily had her own terms. She refused to get on board with making you a wizard if she couldn't probe you like she wanted."

"I think we should just get started."

Mallor was over this conversation, hearing again and again about Analise gambling his life to get what she wanted. She was hard not to admire, but she was even harder not to hate.

He found himself detesting her.

"So pick your worst memory and think about breaking that target board." She pointed to the other end of the room, about half a mile away.

"You want me to break it? Shouldn't I be hitting the target in the center?"

"When you have all-consuming power, accuracy is not integral. At least not to the extent that you need accuracy when playing darts, for example." She stood next to him, staring intently at the target next to the one she wanted him to hit. This target, on the left of the room, was metal with a bright-red circle in the center. Less than one second later, the target had shattered, leaving the red circle in the center on the floor with the rest of the metal. "See. The destructive energy covers all the space you need so long as you're on the target in some way."

Mallor shut his eyes.

"What the hell do you think you're doing? How are you supposed to hit the target if you can't see it?"

The scolding pushed him. It was how he was used to being trained. He blinked his eyes open, focused on the red dot of the target in the middle of the room. Clenching his jaw, he thought of poor nights of sleep. He knew that was a negative experience and proceeded to pick up his hand and mimic the waving motion.

When nothing happened, he looked at her confused.

"What memory did you pick?"

"Poor nights of sleep on the hunt."

"That's not a negative event. It needs to be specific."

Mallor thought harder.

"Focus on your dad. The dining table."

"What?"

"I just told you Lily probed your brain. I know it's personal, but you need to use it."

Analise had seen that memory. It was painful for him to think about, and while he was mad at her for violating his privacy, seeing him go through that kind of hurt must have been hard for her, too.

"I'm sorry you had to see that." His voice softened.

What she had been through had been just as bad, if not worse. She struggled with thinking there was no escape from the pain inflicted upon her by her sister. He didn't have that problem. Mallor had always suspected his parents would give him away when they could, even though the hunters always felt like a myth growing up.

"It's okay. That's all in my past now. We're not there anymore."

"Are you ever going to tell me where we actually are?"

Mallor had tossed location to the side in all of his planning, but he was starting to feel a bit discouraged. The fact he was already failing at magic, something he had always assumed those with powers were naturally good at, was not helping him.

"We're not too far away from Leon's, actually. We needed to position ourselves close to you to make sure we could get to you."

"How did you know I was going to be there?"

"Lily can predict what will happen for people so long as she has a piece of them."

"A piece of them? What does that mean?" Mallor was growing anxious at the idea he had been watched. He was more concerned there was something of his they had. He hadn't even realized there was something of his to be had. Quite frankly, he felt best when he had nothing to lose.

"You lost a shoelace when you first came to Cinder." Her voice soured when she mentioned her home.

"I didn't even notice," he muttered back, playing shy but speaking with honesty.

He was wrapped up in the loss of Teil and could have easily missed something like that. Although, the thought had never occurred to him his men shouldn't be leaving belongings at covens during hunts. He wondered how many of them were being tracked. They had never anticipated this during training, and now he had no way of warning them.

"Does something like a strand of hair work?" He couldn't keep himself from pressing on, and he was even more incentivized as Analise looked excited by his intrigue. "Are there more like Lilith?"

"It has to be an object someone is attached to. I didn't think your laces would work, but we tried it. What *do* those dirty laces mean to you? And her name is Lily. She will kill you if you keep calling her Lilith."

He was more anxious at the idea there could be more witches like Lilith. He needed to know who else was in danger of being caught. This could cripple his plan if the original families knew the hunters were coming to the Election. He rambled, eager to change the subject.

"My mother gave me those shoes before I was given to the hunters. They were torn up on the way back from Cinder, so I tossed them before the Court gave me a new pair."

He had realized his mistake in saying too much, but also felt abnormally comfortable with Analise. He didn't trust her by any means, but she put him at ease. He needed to get back to the original question.

"Are there more like Lilith—sorry, Lily?"

"No. So far as we know, she's the only one of her type. Her story is long, and she's never really told anyone how she ended up here."

"Why doesn't she seek power?"

"You mean on her own? Of a coven?" Analise seemed surprised by the question, but Mallor knew if he wielded that kind of power, he would want to build something great. Well, he did wield some of that power now. An odd thought, that was.

"Right. She could do it, couldn't she?"

"I suppose she could. She's always enjoyed being useful to others. I think it's because being a demon has always caused people to see her in a negative light. She just wants to do something good."

"Good? You do remember she nearly killed me, right?"

"Come on. We both know you were faking it."

Mallor blushed at the fact Analise had caught him.

"She wants to be useful," she said, "She's rather lovely if you get to know her."

"I'm okay, thanks."

A moment of silence passed between the two. Analise smiled at his clear distaste, somehow enjoying the moment.

"So I need to dig deeper?"

"Dig into your family, sweetheart."

He blushed again. He was going to have to get used to this if he intended to make her fall for him. Somehow, he knew it was going to be quite the task.

He shut his eyes, zeroing in on the dining table.

"Keep your eyes open."

"I just need a second." He pressed his eyes closed, pushing them until all he saw was black until a picture emerged.

There he was: a child who had never seen war. He looked at the light-brown legs of the chair in front of him, feeling the table rumble above him. The floor sounded with crashes of pots and pans and screams from his mom that caused him to wince. Helpless, but more than that—angry. He had not killed anyone yet, but if he could, he would have killed his father right then and there. He would have ended this pain for the mother who loved him so much, for the mother who gave him an escape from a life of trauma through giving him up.

He opened his eyes, staring directly at the target in front of him. Mimicking the movement with the wand Analise had shown him, he tugged at the string inside him that held his pain. Fighting to hold onto the hurt instead of pushing it away as he had done for ages, he shouted out as he channeled power into him.

A blue light went through him, going from his heart directly into his hands. It made him cold but also fiery hot as if he were washing his hands under a scorching hot tap after spending the day in the snow.

He gasped as the target in front of him fell to pieces.

CHAPTER 15

———

Mallor stood there in disbelief, shocked at his own abilities. Analise touched his arm, consoling him. He turned to her, looking her in the eyes and falling back into the green as if it were the first time they had met. He melted, seeing in her eyes the same pain he felt. It was as if she had been there, experiencing every second with him.

"Can you see the image in my head when I do...that?" He broke eye contact, looking down at his wand, ashamed of his vulnerability.

"No. But I do know what that pain felt like."

He smiled a sad smile back at her.

She cleared her throat, breaking the silence between them as they shared pain like he hadn't done with anyone else before.

"Now do it again." Her voice returned to being authoritative, seemingly just as uncomfortable with the bond forming between the two of them. She began walking away, confusing him.

"Did I do something wrong?"

A part of him didn't want her to leave. Attributing it to a desire to be coached, he shoved away any thought he might actually enjoy her company and avoiding the solace she provided.

"No. You did that correctly." She stopped in front of the door, one hand on the handle. "Harness it and keep going. I'll see you for dinner."

"But—"

The door shut behind her. He didn't know if he was going to have to relive that memory every time he channeled magic. One thing he was sure of, however, was he couldn't think about that night again and again. At least not without her there.

Mallor stood there, drenched in sweat that cancelled out the shower he had so enjoyed earlier. He had forgotten about Analise and had fixated on the fact he was failing.

The clock on the right side of the wall ticked away the hours as he knew he was missing dinner. He couldn't get it right. It was like he had lost the ability to access bad memories, knowing he had locked many of them away to cope for so long

These memories, the ones that really hurt, had always distracted him when fighting as a hunter. Now, he had to find them again and actually use them to accomplish a goal. It all felt deeply counterintuitive to anything he had ever tried.

Exasperated, he was ready to try again, reaching for a different memory when the door swung open.

"You missed dinner." A quiet, yet familiar voice broke the silence he had stood in for hours. Analise, dressed in a long, dark maroon dress.

He was embarrassed to be seen by her, knowing how much worse he must look.

"You look-"

Before he could call her pretty, she interrupted him in proper Analise fashion. "You need to eat. You have a full day of training tomorrow."

The idea he had to wake up and be bad at magic all over again deflated his spirits.

"Great!" he lied. There was no way she would take him to the Election if he proved useless. He vowed to get it right the first time they ran drills tomorrow, sure a night of rest would fix the problem.

She smiled back at him. "Dinner is in your room. I have business to attend to, but Lina will pick you up at six tomorrow morning."

"Lina?" He wondered what had happened to Lilith. Figuring today was a fluke, he had chosen not to get comfortable with the idea he would be able to avoid seeing her again.

"You seem to prefer Lina." Analise looked down at her hands, playing with her rings. "While I don't usually take my trainees' preferences into consideration, I need you ready to fight in two days. The fewer times you throw a fit, the better."

"That's kind of you." Mallor was properly thankful. He believed she was cruel to most, and she would be to him. Despite the good day they had together, he was no fool to believe he was anything more than a tool to her. She had made that very clear.

"Don't get used to it, trainee."

She gestured for him to leave the room, and they began walking down the corridor.

"I'll never get used to how big this place is."

"Don't you navigate the woods on a daily basis? This is nothing compared to the expanse of the world you scale."

Sounding like it was a compliment, Mallor stood up straighter.

"Sure." He knew they needed to chat more, and missing dinner was a faux pas. While he didn't feel like he had stood her up, he did feel guilty. "Why are you dressed so nicely?"

His voice quieted on the last word, realizing he had complimented her on accident.

She stood in front of him, but he could hear the smile in her voice when she responded. "This is just how I dress. Of course, that is when I'm not scouring for blood." She chuckled, referencing the state of her when they had first met.

"Maybe I should start dressing better."

"Maybe you should."

They arrived at his door and he felt a surprising sadness to be leaving her. "See you in the morning." He lit up at the idea he would see her again. What the hell was going on? Maybe this is just what it felt like to have a friend.

"Oh, and make sure you shower."

Yet again, his face went red. He nodded, responded with a "good night."

The door shut behind him. He realized he was starting to get tired of seeing doors shut when Analise was on the other side. He hopped into the shower, pinching himself to get back on track. Besides, she was the one who he was meant to be fooling.

CHAPTER 16

——

A loud rapping on the door broke the peaceful silence that a restful night had brought him. Checking the bright-white letters glowing on his clock, he realized it was past 6 a.m. and he was likely to have missed breakfast. He groaned, sprung up, and opened the door.

Analise stood in front of him, dressed in her training gear. It hugged every part of her in a way that made Mallor feel guilty for even laying his eyes upon her. Sure she was going to begin chewing him out for waking up late, he braced himself for the wrath that was about to come.

Mallor rambled, hopeful he could fix this mistake before she decided not to take him to the Election for a lack of discipline. "I'm so sorry, I'll—"

Just as he spoke, she began at the same time. "Breakfast is now—"

The two stopped speaking at the same time, goofily smiling at their timing.

As always, she took the lead. "I think it's best if you get dressed. The training room is being fixed up for today's lessons. We have time."

"So I'm not late?" His shoulders fell in relief and his jaw unclenched as his lips grew into a smile at the idea of food.

"No. I told Lina to let you sleep."

She couldn't make eye contact, which confused him. Had he done something wrong? Her eyes fell over his arms and quickly shifted back up, and it was then he realized he wasn't wearing a shirt.

"Thank you. I'll be out in a second." He just about pushed her out of the room, embarrassed by his body. This feeling was odd, as he had changed in front of so many men so frequently. There was something about her seeing him, first thing in the morning with not a single weapon on him that made him feel...exposed.

He changed out of his sweats and threw on a black training shirt and a new pair of black joggers. It wasn't exactly his best look, but it was clean and cohesive. He brushed his teeth in a frenzy, finishing up by running his hands under the tap and washing his face with the water. As he patted his face dry, Analise knocked again.

Reaching for the doorknob, he took a deep breath in to prepare him for the day. He could do this. He could be better than he was last night. She needed to take him to the Election. There was a home he was determined to return to.

The face on the other side of the door, however, disappointed him. Still struck by the beautiful green eyes that seemed to characterize the witches he had recently encountered, he was pushed out the door by none other than Lilith.

His face wrinkled with distaste. "Where's Analise?"

"You have no right to be asking questions given how late you've woken up." Lilith walked quicker than most people ran as she ushered him down the hallways twists and turns. She clearly had no tolerance for his existence, and while her tone might normally ruin his day, he was happy to channel aggression.

Analise was turning him soft and he wasn't really sure how to cope with that. Hating Lilith would be far easier.

"The training room is being cleaned," he said.

"Please. When I first turned, all I did was train. You shouldn't even be indulging in sleep." She looked back at him, glaring. "I thought you were a hunter. Maybe they're not all we're told they are."

"Oh, trust me; we are."

"You *were* a hunter. Now you're nothing." Her words had quickly gone from playfully cruel to downright mean. "Train harder if you want to be something here. We don't keep people around when they have no use."

"Hm. You must think I'm useful if I haven't been tossed out yet." He hinted at her prediction abilities. "Or maybe you're just not that great at predicting the future."

She said nothing in return and merely opened the doors to a living room. She just about threw him into the room, clearly done with spending time in his presence. The feeling was mutual.

He forgot entirely about her existence when he set foot onto plush, white carpets, feeling the softness between his toes after he took off his training shoes at the door. In the center of the room sat a large sectional, looking like a marshmallow that could swallow him in comfort. On the coffee table sat books upon books, and the front of the room had a television playing a cartoon. The dining table was set with pastries and pancakes, food Mallor hadn't even allowed himself to think about since leaving home. Or maybe even since he first learned how poor his family was.

He stood awkwardly at the entrance, unsure of whether this could possibly be for him.

Analise emerged from the kitchen, still in her training gear but holding syrup and peanut butter. "Why are you standing there?" She looked at him, tilting her head sideways in confusion. "You do know you can sit, right? We don't have all day."

"Right, sorry." Mallor's words came out mumbled, unsure how to process his gratefulness for food and his discomfort in being taken care of.

She placed a plate in front of him, and he began circling the rim with his finger. The light flowers on the plate were a good distraction, and he counted the petals of the lilies to avoid her eyes.

Analise sat directly across from him at the circular dining table, and after a brief moment, she began putting pancakes on his plate. "Have you never eaten breakfast with others before?"

"I have. Just not like this. It's all a bit formal."

"Formal? It's just breakfast." Analise seemed let down, clearly excited about the food.

"Sorry. It's not personal to the cooks or anything. The food looks great. I guess I just haven't eaten at a table in a long time."

"There are no cooks. I made this food."

"What?" He couldn't believe she would make this kind of effort just to eat one meal. Where did the resources even come from?

"Would you feel better if we sat on the sofa?"

Mallor looked up from his food, shifting his focus from watching the butter melt over his pancakes to what she said. It was almost as if she wanted him to feel at ease. At home.

His guard shot up. This would never be home and he knew it.

"This doesn't have to be a big deal. We can just watch a cartoon while we eat." She repeated her suggestion, clearly trying to normalize their time together.

He promised himself this would not be home. That didn't mean, however, he couldn't enjoy his time there. He nodded. "Okay."

Together, they moved the books off the coffee table and set up the food, plates clinking on the glass. They sat next to one another on opposite corners of the sectional. They sat feet apart, but the distance didn't keep him from feeling any less nervous.

The TV was loud, and a mouse chasing a cat played on the screen. The show may have been entirely silent and looked rather old, but the two chuckled. He was thankful she didn't try to speak to him again. Mallor was unsure of what he would say, and even more unsure of what he wanted to say to her.

———

They left their dishes on the table, as instructed by the maid who stood by the doorway. They were headed to training now as Lina swung the doors open telling them the setting up of the room was over. Seeing a witch would never feel good to him, but Lina ushering them to training felt like heaven. He may suck at training right now, but he sucked even more at eating a meal with a girl. With Analise.

The sight of the training room in all of its glory—black walls, hard floors, and targets laid about—jolted Mallor out of his head. He felt grounded, and the anger in him was already starting to build again as he remembered his hours of poor performance.

Analise had walked to the other side of the room, gesturing toward the targets he had hit last night. "You'll start with breaking the targets. After you warm up, we'll work on teleportation." She laughed at the shock on his face. " I was going to wait to teach you but we might not have time tomorrow. The reality of this fight is you need to know how to hit and how to move. That's it."

"Why is that it? What if I need to heal or trap someone?"

"That's not your job. Your job is strictly to be on the offense, striking and moving as quickly as you can. I'll take care of the rest."

Mallor didn't enjoy her taking over. He was used to minimizing the role of others, not his own. Being one of those people who strongly believed things could only be done correctly if he was doing them, Analise's comment rubbed him the wrong way. Eyes on the mission, he had to remind himself sucking up his pride was the only way he could get back home.

"Okay. How does teleportation work?"

"Start by warming up. I'll sit behind the glass there," she said and pointed to the wall to the right of him. Apparently, it was a screen through which she could see.

He was shocked, and felt a bit violated he couldn't see the room on the other side.

"Was there someone there yesterday?" he asked.

"When? After I left?"

Mallor nodded in response, his face growing hot at the idea she had seen him screw up repeatedly for hours.

"No. We had a coven meeting."

"Okay. So just a bad memory, right?"

"A cruel memory always works better," Analise answered bitterly, and turned to the wall through which she would watch him.

The wall split, a screen revealing itself. She stepped through it, landing on the other side. Mallor could no longer see her, but he knew she was there staring directly at him. He could feel her eyes on him.

He shut his eyes, doing his best not to psych himself out by reliving the helplessness he felt last night. His focus was on doing this right, and a part of him knew this determination came from a desire to impress Analise and not himself. It wasn't like he'd keep using magic once he left. He'd have to hide himself, and that meant giving up everything he would learn here. Doing this right, however, was his ticket out of here.

He had tried different memories last night, but they had proven futile. He was just going to focus on this one until he could pick a different moment, because at the rate he was thinking about this, he could quickly grow indifferent to the memory.

This time, there was no struggle. It was as if he was suddenly fully capable of finding the string where the memory sat and tugging it to channel his magic.

The board in front of him broke immediately. Without stopping to cherish the moment, mostly due to fear it would give away the fact he hadn't been able to do this yesterday, Mallor continued to hit the two targets to the right of the middle one. They broke in a swift wave of the wand, and he dropped the wand to try the two on the left with merely his hands. Both targets shattered, coming down with one wave of his hand.

His body filled with power and he was overwhelmed by joy. A night of rest had helped. Well, he assumed that was what made a difference. The feeling of being invincible overjoyed him, and he grinned like an idiot at the damage he had caused.

Analise appeared next to him again, smiling. "Congrats. I guess the few hours of practice last night really did help you."

"Oh, it was the pancakes that did all the work." Mallor turned and smiled at her, his eyes lingering to absorb the sparkle in hers.

Analise turned to point to the targets, breaking the moment. "You will go from where you are standing right now to there."

"We're already starting with teleportation?"

"Of course. We leave tomorrow night for the Election. You need to be ready."

"Okay. How do I do it?"

"Movement is different than destruction. It is reliant on hope. You need to think about a time you have been excited for your future and excited for what is to come."

"And if I've never felt like that?"

"Trust me, you have. Everyone looks forward to being somewhere. Whether that be your glee when first seeing the deer you thought could give you strength to get back to Leon's, or whether it be coming home from school and being excited to see your mother."

"Fair enough." Mallor considered taking a risk with his next question. "What do *you* think about?"

"What?"

"What gives you hope?"

Analise breathed in sharply and he was almost worried he wouldn't get an answer from her.

"Leaving Cinder."

"What did you think about before you left?"

"Leaving Cinder. It's always been about that."

"Right. Well I'm glad you left that hellhole."

She looked at him surprised his verbal distaste sprawling across her face.

It was rare they were on the same side, but he felt good about it. He meant what he said. Witch or not, she deserved better than what her sister had inflicted upon her.

"Anyway." She moved a foot away from him, and he wondered if it was intentional or merely for functionality. "Think about going somewhere, anywhere, and hone in on that feeling. The excitement of moving, of going forward."

"That's it? I just have to...think?"

"Of course not. Once you let the happiness of movement overwhelm you, you picture your destination. Then, you shut your eyes and jump straight up."

Mallor couldn't contain his laughter. "What, like a bunny?"

Analise clearly did not find this nearly as funny as he did. She stood there, face stone cold. "No. Bunnies jump forward." Hearing the hilarity of her statement, she began to giggle.

"We have to get this right."

"Right. I'll think about—"

"Don't tell me!" Analise quickly interrupted him as if they were children making a wish in a well and Mallor was about to reveal what he wished for.

"What! Is that a real problem?"

"No, but it is to me! Superstitions are real, you know." She laughed at her childishness and ushered him to continue with the spell.

Mallor smiled, enjoying her company as she finally seemed like a normal person. But she *wasn't* a normal person. She had taken his life from him. He couldn't help but feel conflicted because everything she had done since then had been for his comfort and joy. Then again, she was just using him.

His expression faded. He wanted to get this spell right. It could even be useful as he tried to get away during the Election.

He thought about the first time he heard rumors of the hunt. While at the time he was oblivious to the fact parents gave up their children, and even more oblivious to the harsh nature of the job, he knew in his heart it was where he belonged. He turned into that feeling and the idea he might finally have somewhere in this world that was meant for him.

Fifteen-year-old Mallor was decent at most things but hadn't found his calling like many of his peers had. As they leaned toward medicine and technical subjects, he felt deeply in limbo. He felt ready to finally have somewhere to look. He found solace in knowing he had somewhere to go.

He shut his eyes, swallowing how silly he felt at the prospect of springing into the air. Given it was for the greater good, he pushed himself off the floor and jumped and gravity shifted. It was as if he were being pushed forward, which in a sense, he was. He landed on his feet, but quickly collapsed as he blinked his eyes open. He was on the opposite side of the room. He stumbled to his feet.

Analise stood across from him, staring as if he had done something wrong.

"Look! I did it!" He was too excited to address her expression. Moving without effort, being merely pushed to where he needed to go and honoring thoughts of joy; he was sure there was nothing better in the world.

"Yes. You did." Analise's voice was stern but showed clear notes of confusion.

"What's wrong?"

She was so good at snagging every second of happiness he had, and he found himself resenting her, as if all the hurt she had caused him was compiling and manifesting at once.

But the time for restraint had passed. He was angry and seething through his teeth. "Hello! What's wrong? I did that fantastically and you're just standing there with nothing to say."

"You just seemed...*happy*. It threw me off. Most people hate teleportation and normally puke on the first try."

"Well, maybe it's just something I'm good at."

"Maybe." Analise shifted as Mallor began walking back to her from the other side of the room. "I'm going to go. Keep working on teleporting, starting with the four corners of the room, and run yourself back and forth as much as you can."

"Can't I try to go somewhere else?" While he felt deflated at Analise's underwhelming response, he really wanted to see where else he could go.

"The training room is fortified with charms. It means you can't leave it magically."

"And if I wanted to leave generally?"

"Lina will be watching you behind the wall. I'll see you in a few hours for dinner."

Analise moved out of the room so quickly Mallor had no time to protest. He wanted her to stay, even just to spend more time flirting after their little tiff. He sure as hell hadn't instilled in her enough trust for her to give him time alone once they arrived at the Election. If he were to escape and find his clan, she needed to trust him enough to let go.

The time passed quickly. He continued to run drills, trying to keep his mind off of her comment. Hearing "You looked happy," was not exactly kind. While it sounded like a compliment, he wondered if she saw him walking around sulking all day. Was that really what she thought of him?

CHAPTER 17

He shook his head, trying to rid her from his thoughts. At least he saw her as talented, something he was starting to accept. Continuing to run back and forth in the room until he became dizzy, he heard a knock.

"Come in!"

Whoever was on the other side of that door was going to come in regardless of what he said. Accrediting it to a force of habit, he awaited to see who would show up this time.

"Well done, Mallor." Lina strolled into the room, looking genuinely impressed at his progress.

"Thanks. I have to say, a short break is relieving." Mallor was breathing a bit heavy and reached for his water bottle on the floor of the training room. "Is it always that tiring?"

"You'll grow endurance over time. It's a lot like training for the physical aspects of the hunt." Lina began speaking in Mallor's terms, something he found great comfort in. "You get better and better over time."

Being better at something, even if it was magic, lit a fire in Mallor's heart. Self-improvement being the crux of where he focused all of his bitterness, he was thrilled there was space for progress. He had almost let himself forget he wouldn't have these resources for much longer. Almost.

"Good to know." His mind shifted from dehydration to hunger as his stomach growled over his speaking.

"You seem hungry. Let's get you fed."

Mallor tilted his head at the idea someone else was feeding him. The last person to call him for dinner was his mother, and Lina's maternal nature was foreign to him. He would have to leave the possibilities of magic behind tomorrow when he returned to the clan, but he was going to allow himself to embrace being taken care of. After that, it was back to rare showers and hungry fighting. Just as he liked it.

He wondered what they would serve.

Oh. Oh no. He quickly turned his head, looking at her questioningly, one eyebrow raised. He didn't particularly trust the witches to feed him. Them trying to feed him is what got him here in the first place. All sense of warm nostalgia he had disappeared.

She caught his eyes and giggled. "We don't only eat people, you know."

Mallor sighed in relief, unclenching his jaw.

"We just eat them sometimes." She smiled and winked, sending chills down Mallor's spine as he gave her a sour smile in return.

The walk to the dining hall felt odd now that Mallor knew he could move in other ways. He diverted his attention by investing in the small talk with Lina, hearing about her day.

He had just assumed she played a role in the security of the coven. Given she had imprisoned him, that was the only role he could see her in. It turned out she was Analise's second in command and far too soft to be on security duty full time.

She cared deeply for the people Analise had brought from Cinder and believed with her whole heart in the liberation of witches from hiding. She wanted to improve human and witch relations, not just for the general ease it would bring but because she missed her mother. She mentioned her mother having dementia, and she had hoped becoming a witch would give her the powers needed to reverse the pain her mother felt. It hadn't worked.

It was on that note she gave Mallor a sad smile and opened the dining room doors. He peered into the empty room adorned with golden lights and completed by a long table. The room was filled with people—waiters running around with bottles of wine and guests chatting away—but there was no sign of Analise. Without her, he felt out of place. He was sweaty, still in training gear, and had no idea where he was supposed to sit.

Lina, sensing his confusion, piped up. "Don't worry. It's the leaders of the coven. Think of it as the equivalent of the Court of Five in your clan."

"Why are they here?"

"They want to get to know you."

"Why?" His concern was very clear, and he detested he was readable.

"Analise speaks very highly of you."

"Why would she do that?" Mallor was surprised at the thought of Analise thinking about him.

"Because you'll help us win tomorrow, of course."

"Oh. Right." His excitement escaped him, but he quickly recovered before Lina could notice. "Where do I sit?"

"Right here." She pulled out the chair in the middle of the left side of the table.

The room fell quiet, and his chair screeched as he scooted closer to the table. The second he settled, the bustling of the room started back up again. Long wooden tables and chairs juxtaposed against the dark-purple curtains that covered the floor to ceiling windows blew him away. Everything looked spotless, each bowl, plate, and piece of cutlery glistening in silver.

"Wine?" Lina asked.

"Um...sure." Normally he would never hesitate to turn down alcohol, but the food being served on his plate combined with the intrigued smiles of the witches around the table made focusing on any questions posed to him very difficult.

"So Mallor, is it?" the woman to the right of him addressed him. She was in a purple blouse, silky and nearly so reflective he could see himself in it.

"Yes." While he put up with enough being kind and civil to witches who had been raised to hate, there was no way they would be getting anything out of him.

"Reserved, are we?"

This witch was getting on his nerves. Her tone was condescending and unkind, not at all welcoming for a newcomer and especially not for someone who strongly disliked them.

"Stop bothering the boy, Sarah." A high-pitched voice spoke up from across the table.

"I'm not a boy." Mallor flushed red as he played his childish remark back in his head. His mom would be on him if she heard him speaking this way, but she was nowhere in sight.

The witch across the table laughed at his remark. She was surprisingly warm, which threw him off and only made him feel worse. "I'm Kel. It's nice to have you here, Mallor." She glowed as if it were true.

Maybe it was? Maybe they were actually happy to see him.

"Analise has told us a lot about you."

Even if they were happy to see him, it was only because of his utility. *Fair enough*, he thought. His utility was typically where his worth came from anyway.

"That's nice of you. She's kind."

He figured it was time to show some manners, anyway. While he didn't expect Analise to kick him from the mission for being rude, he didn't need to make any more enemies. The more skeptical they grew, the more likely they were to investigate him.

The one to his right looked like she was keen to find any way to drop him.

"She is kind. She's also smart," Sarah remarked. "That's why I was so surprised she chose you."

The backhanded compliment took him back. He knew she was cruel; it was apparent in the way she first spoke to him. It was the insult toward Analise that shocked him.

"She *is* smart," Mallor said. "That's why she chose me."

"Someone's defensive!"

Sarah was starting to tic him off.

"Sounds like you like her, sweetheart?" Kel questioned, her voice not at all ill-intentioned but clearly accusing him of something.

"They say men sleep with people to get where they want." Sarah laughed at her own comment.

"Excuse me?" Mallor was deeply confused at her insinuation.

"That's the only reason someone like you'd be here. Pretty face and all."

"What?"

"Stop acting so damn shocked. We can all see it. The way she arranged the best room in the coven for you," Kel droned on about Mallor and Analise.

His mind reeled.

"Mallor?"

"Huh?"

"Are you here to daydream or converse?" Kel questioned him.

"Someone's clearly dreaming about Analise," Sarah snickered next to him.

Mallor looked at her, shooting daggers through his eyes. "It was a joke!"

Kel giggled. "Only if he wants it to be." She winked at him, clearly trying to defuse the tension that had taken over the dinner table.

The rest of the table continued to talk over them and coming back from his zoning out felt like stepping out of a pool after being submerged. The world refocused around him and he figured if he was going to gain control over this conversation he would have to take the reins.

"So how's everyone feeling about the Election?"

"Just fine." The sureness in Kel's voice took Mallor aback.

He wasn't used to the Election being spoken about without doubt, especially not when planning with the clan. The men often acted like they knew what they were doing, but he knew not to be presumptuous even in his encouraging words to the clan.

"Fine?"

"Of course." Sarah finished her drink, sounding almost normal.

He was proud of himself for returning the conversation to a neutral chat.

"Analise has been training for years," she continued. "Even before she brought us from Cinder and varying clans, she was training teams of soldiers. She's an incredible strategist for her age."

That was always what struck him as so shocking. At seventeen, Analise was a born leader. Although he would never admit it, he was in awe of her.

"I didn't realize she had been planning this for so long."

"Oh, of course. She'd never think of killing her family, but she's sure as hell going to knock them down a peg," Sarah continued on, digging away at the food in front of her as she spoke between bites.

Her statement was untrue. He was with her when she had tried to kill her family and felt a bit of pride he was the only one who knew how deep her hatred for Cinder ran. He wondered if anyone knew about the abuse, or if the cause Analise had convinced them to support was reuniting the witches with the human world.

He would not be asking that question today. He also needed to stop thinking about her.

"That's great. What role does everyone here play?"

"Each role is a bit too complicated to delve into within the hour. However, we usually just do what is necessary of us."

"What do you two do, then?" He wanted to keep the conversation focused on them.

"Well, I organize most meetings and events held," Kel said. "Consider me a type of diplomat."

This made sense. She was comforting, and beyond the fact she made Mallor uncomfortable with comments about Analise, he felt relatively safe to speak around her. At least more safe than he felt around Sarah.

"Sarah's a trainer." Kel gestured in Sarah's direction.

"I whip the witches into shape."

Analise had assigned the roles well. If this was any indication of the appointment of the rest of the women at the table, it was clear she had thought it all through. Sarah was aggressive enough to be a trainer and clearly cared very little about what anyone thought about her.

"Normally I'd be working with you," she said, "but Analise was very clear this was her responsibility. Besides, I wouldn't have been nearly as kind to you." She licked her teeth.

"Fair enough. I think I would've been able to handle it, having been a hunter and all." Mallor sipped his water, finally easing up enough to appreciate the food in front of him. The many smells wafted through the room, pies and crumbles smelling sweet. Across the table were various meats and a massive turkey sitting in the middle of the room, reminding him of the human tradition of Thanksgiving. Although his guard was down and he was putting his hunger over his skepticism, he did glance across the spread quickly.

No ominous foods. No human parts. He repeated the words to himself again and again, gazing over each food.

Sarah smiled, clearly impressed by his confidence. "That's what we want to hear. We've got a lot riding on you."

"Don't put that kind of pressure on the boy!" a voice from the other side of the table echoed.

The woman at the head of the table was in a classy cocktail dress. It was clear she held some authority here. It also dawned on Mallor that everyone around him was listening to their conversation, despite how entertained with their own company they seemed.

Mallor had nearly finished eating and checked the time on the clock on the wall. The clock ticked nine o'clock at night, and he was tired of entertaining. After the initial anxiety, the witches ended up being relatively kind. They hadn't necessarily changed his opinion, but he found himself feeling like they were a lot like his friends. Each of them played roles similar to the Court of Five, all prioritizing what was right in this world. If only their methods to hold this power hadn't been as morally questionable, Mallor could see him not hating them.

This realization was also throwing him off. He felt conflicted he didn't hate them as much anymore, and he wondered if that would impact his ability to fight in the Election tomorrow.

He had a mission. A life to get back to. There was no way he was giving it up. It was a lot like naming the fish you had caught with your dad. You knew you were going to eat the fish, but if you named it, eating it only became that much harder.

It helped a bit these witches actually ate real people. Some even did it recreationally, he had to remind himself. Not all the witches were from Cinder. Some came from Iro or other covens that were historically known for drinking so much blood populations died out.

He had to refocus. Getting Analise to trust him entirely before they left tomorrow was at the top of his to-do list. He needed to see her if he were going to be successful tomorrow.

The Election lasted two days, both between ceremonial prep and the battles. The witches were thrown into trick battles, traps challenging them when they least expected it. It would be a few days of death, and Mallor needed her to know he was by her side. Some part of him just wanted to see her.

"Excuse me. I should get some rest before we leave tomorrow." He thanked the witches for dinner, leaving them amicably and trying not to replay some of their crueler comments in his head. He was compromising himself to be digestible, and it was killing him. No matter how "normal" they seemed, they were surely there to put him in his place. They were all playing a game and he saw right through it.

He weaved his way through the halls, impressed by his ability to find his way through this massive space. While he took a few wrong turns, he finally ended up at the door of her office. It had occurred to him on his walk she may be in bed, and he was concerned all this walking was for nothing. He wasn't sure what he would do if she wasn't there.

He placed his fist against the door and knocked three times. He waited, feeling like a little boy. After thirty seconds, he went ahead and knocked again. No answer again. He let himself in, pushing the door against his natural instincts. He knew it was poor etiquette, but he was getting nervous.

The door opened and a little candle on her desk flickered. Papers were scattered clearly indicating the night of work Analise had.

At seventeen, she was one of the most ambitious people he ever met. She let the weight of the world rest on her shoulders, and he was continuously astounded by the grace with which she carried herself through it all. An entire mission of making her own justice. He had never had the courage to properly stand up to his father. Not like this. She amazed him.

He needed to see her.

His stomach turned, and a pit in his stomach formed from her absence as he walked down the hall. He sulked, staring at the floor and dragging his feet when he collided with someone. He quickly looked up and saw Kel on the floor after he had nearly slammed her.

He rushed to help her up. "I am so sorry! I didn't see you there."

She stood up, straightening out her dress and smiling. "Don't worry about it. Were you chatting with Analise?"

"No. I wanted to talk to her about the mission, but she wasn't there."

"Oh, dear," Kel said, disappointed. "I wanted to talk about tomorrow as well. Maybe she's in her room?"

"She's probably asleep."

"Analise? The poor girl rarely sleeps. Come, let's go give her some company. I just need to drop off the map for tomorrow and make sure she knows the schedule."

"Oh, okay."

And off they went.

Kel gave him the rundown of the day. They would be leaving at 11 a.m., most of them teleporting and others using normal human transportation to keep the mission under the radar. They would settle in right outside the Election, and Analise would challenge the witches for the title of Original Witch.

Now that she was no longer associated with Cinder, her eldest sister was up for the title. While the mission was important to Analise, she was looking for the chance to kill her sister.

They continued walking, and Mallor felt in his element. Being told the plan and being integrated into a mission with a real goal made him really begin to feel at home.

They arrived at her door. It was made of black wood and the crowning of the door was coated in gold lines. It was stunning and very fitting for the women who lived behind it.

Kel knocked with no hesitation, not feeling or recognizing the nerves that occupied Mallor's being.

"Who is it?" Analise called from inside, clearly not expecting anyone.

"Kel!" Kel called and pushed the door open at the same time, not bothering to wait for an invitation. She entered the room, leaving Mallor awkwardly standing at the front door.

He wasn't sure whether to enter or not, completely unsure of etiquette in a woman's room. Growing up, he had very few female friends. Before he could make any, he was too busy killing those who had turned into witches. Women weren't really on his radar, and while he was a boy and had puppy crushes on young teachers, he had rarely been faced with the prospect of interacting with them. Not in their room.

He fiddled with his ring, standing there like a little boy.

Kel began to ramble, rehashing everything she had just shown him. She sounded like a little girl accepted into her dream school, rambling on. The future was clearly something she was ready for, and she couldn't hide her child-like joy despite being clearly in her late twenties.

Analise peered around Kel, seeing Mallor was waiting in the doorway. "Oh! Hi."

She seemed a bit...nervous. Maybe having a boy in her room was just as foreign to her.

"Come in! Please feel free to..." She looked around processing the fact there was only one seat in the room. It was white and matched the desk in front of her. She was sitting in the only chair and seemed puzzled.

"Mind if I just sit on the bed?"

The awkward tension between them was causing Kel to smirk, and Mallor was ready for them to finish their conversation so Mallor could start his.

He was exhausted, but the adrenaline in his stomach was desperate to be used. His stomach turned, and he realized this was what his friends from grade school called "butterflies."

He mentally yelled at himself for being a soft sap around a girl when he had very little to do with her. Right? Right. Mallor chalked it up to nerves, knowing a big day was ahead of him.

Analise smiled at him as he sat down. She looked back up at Kel, no longer focused on him. "So where were we?"

The two continued to chat and Mallor spun his ring around his ring finger. He wasn't even sure when he had gotten it, and it didn't mean much to him. He tried not to get emotionally attached to items because they tended to get lost. This was also how he felt about people, a lesson he had quickly learned after losing Teil.

Teil's fate was still unknown. He didn't have time to hash out a plan right now, not between learning magic, getting to the Election, and returning to his clan. If the Election went as planned, he would return to Cinder and check Helena's cell for Teil. It was his only option, and there was no way Teil would be at the Election. Cinder wouldn't risk it and *if* he was alive, he would run as far from the Election as possible.

Kel hugged Analise in his periphery. Their conversation seemed to be wrapping up, and so he prepared himself mentally for a conversation. He wasn't fully sure what he wanted to say; he just wanted to chat.

Kel turned around, facing Mallor. "Have a goodnight, kids. Don't do anything crazy!" She winked at him and walked herself out of the room. The door slammed, but he barely heard it as his face went bright pink.

CHAPTER 18

"So." Analise placed her gaze on Mallor as soon as the door shut quietly behind Kel.

Mallor looked up at her, making direct contact with her green eyes. She had broken the silence and he held her gaze as it brought him back from the embarrassment of Kel's comment. "So?"

"What do you mean *so?*" Analise's tone was bright, happy, and clear. "You're the one who's in my room." She smirked at him.

"Right. I just wanted to chat."

"About the Court dinner?" She seemed concerned. "Did they make you want to leave? It's too late now, anyway."

"No, no. Don't worry. I want to come tomorrow." He cleared his throat. "I'd like to be there for you." He meant it but continued to convince himself the vulnerable comment was merely to gain her trust.

"Sure. The team needs you anyway."

"Right. The team needs me."

"How was dinner, then?"

"Fine. They were kind."

Her smile grew, amused at his kindness even though she knew how harsh the women must have been.

"A little mean, sometimes, but I would feel threatened by me too," he joked, causing her to chuckle and roll her eyes at him.

He laughed with her, already feeling like he could breathe a bit more freely than before. Their laughter settled, creating a warm blanket of joy in the room. It was possible Analise needed a good laugh just as much as he did, if not more.

"How's the planning been going?" He remembered how tired she must be.

"It's good. I'm ready to get there tomorrow and make this happen."

Her voice came out like that of a leader, but Mallor looked at her sympathetically as he knew how difficult seeing her family would be.

"Are you nervous? To see your family and all." He wanted to be specific and ask her about her sister, but he knew it would scare her off.

She sat there, pondering his question. Her eyes grew soft, and her tense body language gave him the answer he had predicted. "Somewhat."

She was shutting down, and if he continued to push her, he would be out of here before he could be sure she trusted him. While he had walked in with no plan, it hit him the only way to be sure of her trust was to get her to spill a secret. This would be a long game tonight.

"I can't imagine seeing my family again." If he opened up, maybe she would too. Nothing he said had to be real, she just had to believe him. This statement, however, was true.

She nodded. "What they did to you was so hard."

"Well, it was just my dad, really." He was starting to tense, the words coming out of his mouth before he could be more tactful.

"No, but your mother never stopped it."

They sat there in silence.

"That's one of the reasons I'm going tomorrow," she said. "My family never stopped it."

"I thought Helena—sorry, your mom—didn't know about...?" Mallor had assumed revealing the abuse committed against Analise would turn all of Cinder against the eldest sister. It was shameful to treat one's own that way in the world of witches. *The Red Book* was clear about that, and while occasions of abuse were swept under the rug, stories that were leaked ruined individuals. Many were pushed back out into the human world, forced to assimilate, and fend for themselves against hunters.

"For a while, she acted like she didn't." She broke eye contact with him, but her words had the same tell. She nervously fiddled with her ring, a small blood-red heart on her right ring finger. "After you left Cinder, I mustered up the courage to tell her what happened. While I didn't want them to die, I needed her to know." She stopped, her breath hitching. Her eyes welled up, and it was clear this was difficult for her to talk about.

Screw the plan. Mallor just wanted to hug the poor girl. He leaned in to show her he was listening. "It's okay. Take your time."

She smiled. Her eyes broke his heart. The first time he had heard of the abuse, his empathy came from hating all abusers. Now, this anger expanded into hatred as he hated not only abusers but anyone who hurt her.

"So I asked her to stay with me in the kitchen after a family dinner. The others had returned to their homes, and she agreed to stay. She wasn't sure what I wanted to talk about and was ready to go to bed. She was irritable."

The last statement was a "caution" sign painted in red that she was trying to hang to ensure he didn't judge her mother, despite the fact her mother deserved the judgment. Leave it to Analise to protect those in her life even when they treat her like dirt.

"I told her what Senali had done to me." She turned away in her chair, too ashamed to look at him. "Her response was it was only the one time, and siblings fought."

"Did you tell her it had occurred more than that? Please tell me how you explained the extent of it." Mallor wanted her to feel powerful enough to share her story. He was rooting for her as she described these courageous steps she took to stop the abuse.

"Yes. I told her the stories. Every moment I could remember. And she banished me."

"I thought it was the abuser who was meant to be pushed out." He tried his best to sound comforting and make her feel supported.

"It is. She told me I was making it up and trying to push my sister from becoming the most powerful witch in Cinder."

"Is that when you left?"

"Somewhat. It's when I began training." Her voice shifted, growing hard and focused. "Both my mother and I knew I could be the most powerful witch. Not just in Cinder but everywhere. The talk about me had been spreading through the covens even before I spoke to my mother, and I knew Senali was jealous."

She wiped under her eyes, collecting the little mascara that had mixed with her tears and created dark circles. "After three months of recruiting quietly to build this coven and training day and night, I challenged my sister to a duel."

"Wow," Mallor said.

Duels between families were rare, and the youngest against the oldest was astounding. He was surprised he hadn't heard about the fight.

"Senali lost. I was chosen as the witch who would fight in the Election soon after. And then, just when they laid out all of their plans and chose a strategy that would only work if I were the one executing it, I left." She smiled, clearly cherishing that moment. "It was liberating." She took a deep breath and let it out.

"I'm impressed." This was an understatement.

While the plan Analise hatched might have seemed elementary, the patience and energy it must have taken to execute it was astonishing.

"Don't sound so surprised. We all know I'm smarter than you, anyway." She teased him, laughing at her own comment.

Acting insulted, Mallor gasped. "How dare you!"

They laughed together, becoming one again after a heavy conversation. While what she had shared was not technically a secret, it was deeply personal. He knew what it took to tell him that, and he was thankful. Not just because he knew he could now trust her, but he was thankful to have been confided in.

"Thank you for telling me."

"Don't worry. I surprised myself by telling you, too."

This made him grin, because while Analise used humor to cope with hard conversations, it was always cute.

"How are *you* feeling about tomorrow?" she asked.

Mallor wasn't sure what honesty he could have with her. "I feel good. A bit nervous, actually."

"About what?"

"Magic is so new to me."

"Mallor, you have learned faster than anyone else I have worked with. Every witch at dinner agreed to meet you because word of what you can do is spreading throughout the coven. You defy everything we know. *The Red Book* doesn't even warn of a wizard."

"What if they're just fascinated by me? That doesn't mean they think I'm good at magic."

He realized how vulnerable he was being and mentally punched himself for letting her in. He promised he would put his guards back up.

"That's not true. Fascination may have been a catalyst to their original interest, but you have kept them invested."

The way Analise said this made him wonder if that was how she felt about him.

He wanted to ask her if she really believed that but didn't want to seem desperate. A need for positive affirmation had never struck him, but with her he just wanted to hear he was good enough.

"So tell me about your day." Mallor changed the subject, both to spend more time gaining her trust and really to just spend more time with her in general. He didn't want to leave yet. While small talk was painful, it didn't even matter to him. Talking to her at all felt like a blessing, knowing just how busy she was.

The two rambled on, chatting about everything from training earlier that day, to what they ate, and to the dinner of the witches. She often teased him, but it was clear every insult she threw his way was really just the opposite of what she meant. The meaner she was, the more he knew she liked him.

While it was a very childish way to express feelings, he embraced it. He hadn't felt like a child in a very long time, and it was lovely to feel like they could be the age they were. No one was forcing them to grow up at this moment, and that was worth cherishing.

She had shifted over to the bed, and the two were now sitting against the headboard, giggling at the cartoons on her television. There was distance between them, and Mallor was growing very aware of the space.

They continued to chat, making fun of the characters and the poor writing. Although it was a great distraction from real life, they were both acutely aware of how human it all felt. There was no magic involved and no hunting. They were just two teenagers enjoying each other's company.

What an odd phenomenon.

They talked themselves to exhaustion, and Mallor began drifting off just as he felt her head fall onto his shoulder. She was asleep, completely unaware of the distance she had closed between them.

Hyperaware of the fact she smelled like roses, he knew he had to get up and leave. He didn't want to go but getting emotionally involved would only hurt both of them tomorrow. Feeling guilty about his plan to fool her, he just knew their night was over.

He slowly shuffled out of bed, careful not to wake her. He set her head against the pillow, taking a quick look. He blushed at her. While she was often confident and focused, two things that made Mallor crave being with her, she was also pretty. Her features were soft, and her hair sprawled across the pillow. She made a little noise when he put her to bed, but turned to the other side of the room.

As she slept no longer facing him, he smiled. Unsure what propelled him, he walked over and gave her a light, swift kiss on the forehead.

His nerves were pumping. Letting himself out of the room, he shut the door quietly and said goodbye to one of the greatest afternoons he had experienced in a very long time.

CHAPTER 19

For once in his life, Mallor felt competent at something he was made for. While he wasn't thrilled about being a wizard, it was oddly consoling knowing he was the only one who existed.

As he walked through the corridor late at night, he took in the little lights that illuminated his path from the floor crown moldings. He smiled to himself, a warmth through his body and unfamiliar pride for what he had accomplished running through his veins. Her excitement for his progress had given him so much joy, and he realized just how long it had been since he last had any positive affirmation.

He knew he could do this. Continuing to remind himself how good tomorrow would be, the small, sad pit building in his stomach confused him. He had everything figured out. Analise was opening up to him just as he wanted, and he had fallen into the good graces of the court. The lines of anxiety in his stomach continued to intertwine. She trusted him. But...did she like him?

He shook off the thought, trying to focus on getting back to the room. Somewhere along the way he had made the accident of befriending Analise. It was time to come to terms with the fact he would be leaving in less than twenty-four hours.

Looking forward into the empty hall and staving away thoughts became easy but removing the odd desire to stay in this place was not. He had grown oddly comfortable here in just a few days, navigating the space with ease in a way he didn't believe was possible. He often ran into people he knew, and more often than not, if it wasn't Lilith, he didn't hate seeing a kind face. And the showers were great, too.

A shower. The thought was deeply appealing after a long night. Hopefully, he could just wash away the guilt. He was ashamed of enjoying himself. Realistically, the bad parts of going back to being a hunter hadn't hit him. The long months, the lack of a warm meal for what felt like ages, the stagnation. While he loved hunting, he hadn't learned something new for a long time. The exhilaration that came with being good at something for the first time showed him just how jaded he was. He had to go back, but did he *want* to go back?

That jolting thought was cut off by Mallor reaching his front door. Opening it on his own, just the way he had been shown on the first day, he chose to forget this conflict. He was going home tomorrow. That's why he had done all this work. That's why he put up with those who he had been raised hating. There was no changing him, and that was clear now. He was just tired and the exhaustion was getting to him. A warm shower that smelled like eucalyptus and a night's rest would do him good.

His worries melted away with the shower as he shut his eyes and let his worries fade. He had spent so much of his life worrying away every good thing.

Tonight was pleasant. He enjoyed his time with Analise, and while he still detested her for everything she had made him into, she had also brought out good things in him. He had someone to open up to, and just a few days of being around her vulnerability was refreshing. It was also enough.

After having stood in the shower for an hour, he cozied himself under the covers. His mind running, his body was exhausted and quickly took over. Sleep had finally come his way, though it was tumultuous.

All he could see was her. Taking in his surroundings, he was unsure where he was. He was on a porch and it was bright white. He stood there awkwardly, confused on where to go. He saw Analise sitting in the yard in front of him. A picnic basket was sprawled out and the sun was reflected on her. Her dress was beautiful. It was light blue and flowy, the ends laying out on the picnic blanket. It was the most perfect day he had seen, as if it were something out of a movie.

As he took her presence in, a voice called from around the corner.

"Mallor! Let's go! Dinner's ready."

Teil, with a smile wide across his face, beckoned him into the home. The home looked like the ones he passed growing up. Every day on his walk to school, he would walk through a neighborhood. He stopped looking once he was old enough to realize that money funded those homes, but he grew up admiring them. The porches, much like this one, were filled with old, wooden rocking chairs in front of big, brick homes. He imagined himself living there and being walked to school like the rich kids from grade school. He imagined a family who knew when school ended or what classes their children were taking.

"Teil?" Mallor ran over, throwing his arms around his friend. "How are you here?" It all felt real. In the back of his mind, Mallor knew this was a dream. But for now, he was going to lean into the peace this moment afforded him.

"Hey, man?" Teil's tone was inquisitive, implying Mallor's excitement was abnormal. He composed himself.

"Hey. Yeah, sorry. Just excited to see you."

"Fair enough. It is your birthday after all, so I suppose I can hug you," Teil joked and lightly punched his arm.

Mallor tried to recollect the last time he celebrated his birthday. He used to love his birthday at the end of April just when spring would hit its peak and the lines of spring lemonade stands blurred with swimming in the community pool.

"Mallor! Hey!" Teil beckoned him inside the house. "Come, let's grab the food. Analise is waiting outside."

"Analise?"

"Yes, of course." He stuttered on his words, looking around the house and admiring the stairs. It was the most suburban home he had ever seen, and after years of teaching himself to hate them, he remembered just what it felt like to be a little kid wanting to be in the home so badly.

"It looks great, doesn't it?"

"What?"

"Analise's renovations. I know she wanted to build out more space for you all to train—"

"Train?"

"Yes? You've been getting really good actually." Teil collected the dishes from the kitchen, scents swirling together, smelling incredible. "I'm so happy she invited me here. It's great to see you guys."

"What type of training are we talking about?"

"Dude, you act like you've forgotten you're a wizard."

"You know?"

"Of course I know! I'm the first person you told when you and Analise escaped the Election."

"Escaped?"

"Come on dude, let's go out and see your girl. She's been setting up all day to celebrate."

Mallor jolted up. He was discombobulated, but all he wanted was for the dream to have been true. Seeing a pretty world in front of him and a woman he cared for with his closest friend, he had experienced acceptance in that dream. Teil knew who he was—*what* he was—and was still there celebrating his existence.

That kind of unconditional love did not exist.

With vulnerability came only shame, and he couldn't forget it.

In a sleepy haze, he looked around his bedroom to grab his belongings. Remembering he had nothing, he chucked a pair of pants, shoes, and a training shirt on. Going to the training room was the healthy way to deal with the reality that had been ripped from him. He told himself to shut up. He needed to go. All of the luxury and encouragement Analise had been sprinkling him in made him weak. He had grown comfortable.

He was losing sight of who he was. He had become every-thing he hated.

It was time to go.

He slowly walked out of his room, picking up the pace once he passed the door frame. Seeing the cells and the room in which he was tortured, he took off sprinting for what looked like the front door.

Analise would never see him again. He envisioned being in the town, close enough to navigate his way out of this hellhole. A voice screamed in his head to turn back, but he was a coward if he stayed and a coward if he left. He could only do what he had grown up knowing, and that was to hunt.

Thinking of the dream gave him hope, and he teleported away from there. Away from her.

CHAPTER 20

—

He landed with a thud, the cinder blocks breaking his fall. Mallor groaned, an ache on his back where a bruise would inevitably develop. His faith in himself and in his abilities had gotten him away, but they did not make him graceful.

Panic was the first emotion to hit him as he realized what he had done. He had left Analise. He had left his clan. He was alone. *Where am I?*

He pushed himself to his feet, hauling his legs forward and hoping the pain wouldn't migrate to the rest of his body. Surveying the room, there were only four walls of cinderblock and a small window. A glimmer of hope ran through him and he moved, forgetting the concept of pain, to the outside world.

Expecting darkness, as it was likely still night, his heart fell when he looked out. The window was merely decorative. It was a single square in the middle of the wall with a window frame bordering the edges, looking out into nothing.

How stupid is this place?

He rolled his eyes and began walking toward the door to leave. When teleporting, he hadn't pictured a place to go to in the town. He had just assumed *out of his room* would be enough. Knowing it would be likely unsafe, he pushed away any warning in his mind that would keep him from continuing his journey.

After a slight moment of anxiety over the door being locked, he was able to push it open. The hall was dim, lit only by little lamps mounted to the wall. It looked nearly medieval which was shocking as the modernity of witch covens was world renowned.

He walked through it, grateful the hall did not have the many twists and turns of Analise's home. The place seemed like a home. There was a little set of white doors he passed, which were clear glass panels with a cozy library and a desk.

Right before the front door was a sectional in a room. The floors inside had plush carpet and seemed oddly familiar. Quietly, he pushed the door open. Not a squeak. He smiled to himself, proud no one saw him.

He hoped to spot what time it was through the potential rising of the sun over the town. His look did not last long. A pang went through his chest.

It was the chair. The wooden chair from the porch in his dream.

Where am I?

He had somehow managed to teleport to this home, one he had made up in a dream. It wasn't even supposed to exist.

How does it exist?

The wind had picked up around him and was hitting his face as he ran. He knew his cheeks were going red, the tip of his nose freezing as he ran through the town. He didn't stop once to fully process the blurs of stores. Running aimlessly, looking for some freedom, he stopped only as the thoughts of fear and confusion inhibited him from moving further. The Election was soon, and he had to figure this out.

Stopping, he caught his breath. The light of a store behind him illuminated where he stood and he faced the main street, trying to find any sign of location. Having no luck, he turned around to face the store.

His heart stopped. It was the very store he had once seen Analise at. It couldn't be. It must have been a rendition of where they had first met. The same fluorescent lights stood out on the front, and the shelves of blood were packed.

Blood.

He never thought he would understand the disgustingly immoral craving of the witches, but he was surely figuring it out. Part of him felt...*parched*. It was completely unexplainable. It felt nothing like hunger, especially because his stomach was just as full as it was after the huge feast with the witch court.

He needed to walk in, as though the lights showcasing the various types of blood were physically drawing him in.

It couldn't hurt him to just step inside and relive that first day he met her. Remember what it was like to be a hunter with a mission that would benefit the greater good of the world.

It probably wasn't even open. Well, he'd let fate decide if he were meant to go in.

The smell of the blood inside was intoxicatingly attractive, like a fragrance store. He pushed. The door wouldn't budge.

He tried again. Pushing harder this time, he found himself only taken with the need to get in. It was like he had never had water and was dying for a sip. He pushed a third time. A fourth. Nothing.

Finally, he kicked the glass with his foot.

The door shattered, each piece falling to the ground loudly. He cursed to himself, realizing what he had done. Pathetic. He was pathetic. Everything he had ever stood against had gotten a hold on him and had taken over. He felt out of control, as if no part of his past life had ever existed. Going into the store was meant to jog his memory, and instead it had only made him realize how every memory he had ever experienced was lost to him.

He fell to his knees, the devastation and sadness falling over him. For once, there was no anger. Tears fell from his eyes and he mourned the life he had once had. He mourned the person he once was. He cried for the life of cannibalism he had succumbed to and the girl he had lost. He cried for a childhood torn away from him, cried for the mother who had given him up to protect him. He didn't know if she was alive or dead, and there was a chance he'd never find out. Shame and guilt washed over him.

An alarm began to ring. Louder than anything he'd ever heard before, it blasted through his thoughts. Incapable of moving, in shock, he continued to sit lonely on the pavement floor, waiting for it to end.

He heard shouting, running. It was getting closer to him. He had to *move. He had to move now.*

His mind and all of his hunter instincts taking over. He shot up, sprinting straight toward the door. Pushing himself through it, the remaining sharp glass cutting his arms, he scurried through the store to hide.

He took a page out of Analise's book and hid behind the register desk. Pulling his knees in close to him, he sat in a ball and put his head between his legs. It was like being under his father's dining table, waiting for the world to fall apart around him.

He was hurting and for the first time in his life, he actually felt it. All he could do was sit there, unsure of his ability to teleport and unwilling to take himself back to the home from his dream earlier.

An eon passed and the alarm did not stop. He did not stop shaking in fear but remembered Teil's training.

"Convince yourself otherwise," he had said. "Fear is not a useful emotion."

Mallor relaxed his jaw and tried to stabilize. He wasn't ready to stand up just yet, but he could remind himself of where he was. He wasn't in his father's home. He was in a coven, hiding, which was something he had done plenty of times before. If anything, he was stronger now. *I can do this.*

Two minutes passed. Then five. Then ten.

He would look over the register, see if there was anyone there. If not, he would get out as soon as the alarm stopped. The paranoia and anticipation of not being able to see what might come for him was far worse than if he were in a real fight.

He stood up slowly. And then, a line of fire came his way.

CHAPTER 21

———

The world lit up in fireworks as fire from witches came soaring into the store front. As the glass front of the store shattered, Mallor's world went with it. The broken door had enabled him to find a safe haven for a bit, but every suspicion he had about whether the commotion was related to him was being confirmed with every passing second.

He must have set off an alarm when he broke into the store. *Shit.*

How was he so stupid? He should've left before they got there. Instead, he sat there wallowing, just hoping it would pass. *Nothing* just passed. He would always have to fight.

His optimism had led him to believe the sirens were for something else. Luck only existed where Analise was protecting him. He would forever be unlucky, and unless she were fighting for him as if he were a pathetic baby, he would never find himself in a good situation. Especially not while in a coven.

Fighting was clearly the only option here as he was far from recalling any happy memories to use. Harnessing all of the despair he experienced, in addition to the resulting trauma, everyone there was a glowing-red target in Analise's practice room.

One deep breath.

He stood up, reaching for his wand. He didn't have one on hand; the time had come to figure out how the witches used their hands to conduct magic.

The only way to learn was to do.

Adrenaline kicked in as the witches approached, nearly snarling as their eyes all glowed that signature bright green. While he would love to stop and reminisce over Analise's eyes, there was no kindness in these faces.

He dodged each shot, cowardly shifting back and forth around the store instead of risking using his magic. If he tried to channel his magic into his hands and it didn't work, this was it for him. He would never see the clan again. He would never see the team of witches who had trained him.

While both teams had drastically different goals, Mallor couldn't afford to disappoint either side of his life.

Somehow, the witches had become important to him. Not all of them, of course. For all he cared, Lilith could still rot away in a hole. It was the ones who cared for him through these few days: Analise, Lina, and even Kel. They had shown him respect. And while he wanted desperately to go back to the life he once had, there was a high chance he would have died in the woods that day. While he would forever regret eating another human—he shuddered at the thought—it had kept him alive. It had given him a second chance at life.

He didn't doubt for a second he would be returning to his clan tomorrow, but he was grateful to be doing it stronger than he was before. Even if the clan would never know what he had become, he knew he was even more capable of killing the witches. The thought surprised him as his mission had felt so far away for so long. Right now, the witches he had to take down were standing right in front of him, trying to kill him.

He kept his eyes open, hoping to hit the witches with a large enough stride it would wipe out the first row around him. He tried to recall what it was like sitting under the table fearing his father.

He unleashed his sadness as much as he could, returning to the shaking little boy he once was. The memory itself was rather blocked out. He remembered how he felt, and it was as if he were looking at himself from the outside in. He watched as little Mallor, untamed brown hair and tears clouding his eyes, tried to contain labored breaths from the sobbing. He noticed his younger self unable to breathe, trying to repress the hiccups that came with poor oxygen intake. His heart twinged for the boy he once was.

And just when he thought there was hope for him, nothing happened.

That was his saddest memory. It *had* to work.

He tried again, continuing to dodge shots at the same time.

And then a strike of fire went through his arm, and his opposite arm shot up to grab the wound. It burned harshly, stinging his skin. It must have been the fact his magic was concentrated in his arms because the searing pain didn't compare to hits from witches during his time on the hunt. At that moment, he missed Lilith's experiments.

He crumbled, as another shot came at him. It was over. There was no fighting his way out of this. There was no court to help him, no Teil to take the blow for him, and no one else to save him. The world shook, as if he were really under his father's dining table. Becoming a shell of a man, he fell into himself and put his head down. Shots continued to come, and three more later, he was sure his skin had been burned off.

He tried to find detachment and remove himself from the emotions of the situation, but it was impossible. In his last moments, all he would feel was shame. And that in itself made him ashamed.

A shout rang through the store, followed by the fall of every witch around him. Mallor's eyes were still closed, and it was only the voice he would recognize in all of this chaos.

"He's with me!"

Analise's voice boomed, commandeering the witches. When she spoke to Lilith, Lina, or even the court, all he heard was softness coated in sternness. She demanded to be heard in any room, but this time around the demand was not to be messed with. Her shout put fear into Mallor's bones, and he couldn't imagine those inferior to her would dare defy her.

He kept his eyes shut, wounded as fire shots had hit him. The sound of witches around him had faded; all were on the floor from Analise's clearly debilitating blow directed at them.

The store grew quiet, and he sat there with his head between his knees, sure she would just leave him alone.

Instead, her footsteps came closer and her breath brushed him and he flinched.

"It's okay. Hey." She spoke to him, no harshness in her voice. It was as if she had just walked in to hug him, and her anger had never existed.

Her voice was soothing and coated in honey.

He wanted so badly to open his eyes and look at her, but he knew the second he fell into her green eyes the guilt would come crashing down. He had run from her after all she had done for him. How was he supposed to tell her that?

She was going to hate him, and the first person he felt that close to would disappear from his life. He pressed his eyes closed even harder.

"Mallor. Please." A pleading entered her voice and she settled on the floor next to him. There they sat, with witches no longer conscious around them, in silence.

The silence itself was desperate; she was clearly disheartened.

Without opening his eyes, his voice came out in a pathetic squeak. "Are you mad at me?"

She took in a sharp breath, pausing before she answered. Mallor braced himself. "Why would I be mad at you?"

He opened his eyes, looked at her confusedly. She seemed genuinely taken aback by his question. "Because," he said, equally as befuddled. "I left."

His voice went nearly silent on the final word, *left*. Heat rushed to his face as he had unsuccessfully run away. It felt like, since the day they first met, he was protecting her. It wasn't until right in this moment, as she smiled a silly smile back at him and wrapped her arms around him, he realized she was the one protecting him.

"Yes. I'm not sure why you did that."

It wasn't a question.

"Well I—" He tried to answer her anyway, as though he owed her the truth.

"You don't have to tell me." She leaned into his shoulder. "I'm sure it was out of fear, but whatever the reason, you've not run away from me here."

He had no intention of breaking free of their comfortable embrace. He had never felt a moment of peace after violence ensued in his life. It was always a matter of experiencing the pain, both on the battlefield and at home, and getting back up. The only option most days was to continue.

They sat together, both healing from an unspoken hurt, not being forced to continue with the fight.

There was time.

He had never had time on his side before.

He shut his eyes and leaned into her chest, finally not combatting his very real feelings for her. He wasn't sure how they had gotten here, but he was done questioning it. He was done pretending this was something that didn't exist. While it may have started as a plan, although he was pretty sure that was him trying to justify his feelings for her, he had never felt so...safe.

Mallor pulled himself out of her arms, reaching for his worst memory. He had to think quickly if he were to protect her, knowing while her first shot missed bringing her death, it was possible the second wouldn't.

The memory under the dining table no longer worked.

When had he been the saddest?

When the dream ended.

He had acted like the end of the dream had brought him anger because it made him soft, but the reality was the end of the dream made him sad because *it wasn't real.*

He was going to fight for it. Fight for his future.

Channeling the pain that came with leaving Teil and Analise on the front porch of the home he had dreamed of living in, celebrating his birthday as he had never done before, he waved his hand.

The heat flew through his fingertips and put a twitching witch on the floor out cold. She collapsed with a thud, and it was clear this memory had worked. He had a new worst memory, and for once he was thankful for the hurt as it had saved Analise.

"Nicely done." She actually sounded impressed with him.

———

The sun peeked through the windows, coating the room in a kind, blue light. Mallor opened his eyes in a haze, looking at Analise as her hair messily fell across his bare chest.

The reality of the intimacy they shared the night before had barely processed. The experience of being with her, in every capacity, was so new to him. He wondered if she was okay, wanting only to have made her feel safe and cared for.

He stroked her hair. These peaceful moments would be few and far between in the lives they lived. He wasn't sure where things would go from here. He looked at her clothes, light hitting them as they lay on the nightstand next to her, and smiled.

A relationship between a witch and a hunter was unheard of. There were no details anywhere about what life would look like. While some witches would fall in love with human men, the problem of blood cravings plagued the relationships. They often became parasitic in nature, and the relationship ended quickly.

Some witches got bored. They latched onto human men directly after turning, seeking some normalcy from their past life. These were often the women who became witches later in life, and it wasn't until they fully realized a relationship with a human couldn't give them children or their old life back they finally gave up the pipe dream.

He wondered if they could make this work. The thought made him panic. Had they missed the Election?

Not long ago he was asking himself how he was going to kill her. And part of him still stood by the mission. He wasn't sure if he could kill her, but the line of witches had to go. They ate people, and he couldn't just magically forget they made him eat someone too. He had some role to play in that too.

Boy, was he confused.

Analise placed her hand on his chest and looked up at him.

"Hi." She smiled at him, timidly placing a kiss on his lips. Her voice was quiet and nervous, but clearly happy to be there.

They both seemed so worried about ruining the moment. Silence hung between them, and all he could do was what he knew would make them feel best.

He kissed her, remembering how soft her lips felt from that very first kiss the night before. His stomach fluttered, and he wondered if he would ever get used to how she felt with him.

He pulled back, having to use all of his willpower to keep the moment from escalating. He wanted to spend all day in bed with her, but there was a world to save and he was no longer sure whose side he was on.

"Mmm," she mumbled, trying to pull him back. It was clear she didn't want to move either. It was reassuring, knowing she craved his company just as he did hers.

"Ana."

"Analise. Call me Analise."

He whispered into her ear. "Okay, Analise." He beamed, loving he could say her name as if it was his. He had noticed often just how little everyone else used her full name. He used it to tic her off, but now it felt like honey dripping from his tongue as he said it. "Don't we have somewhere to be?"

She rolled over, groaning. The idea of responsibility was equally appalling to him, but they had to deal with the real world. They couldn't stay here forever. Both had thousands of people relying on them for very different reasons, and in an ideal world, they would be able to reconcile their goals and become one.

Realistically, this was impossible. And if it wasn't impossible, it was sure going to be difficult. They were going against all of the laws of nature as the world knew them. *The Red Book* didn't even predict this.

Everything dictated their love couldn't happen, and therefore it was time to pull away. For the time being, he would push the thoughts away and try to enjoy whatever time they had left.

"How much longer do we have before the Election is over?"

She came back over to his side of the bed, sitting up and pulling the sheet up above her chest. "They relocated. The Metamorphosis couldn't occur in the old location, so Iro's coven is holding it now."

"Isn't it illegal for a coven to host the Election? Home field advantage and all that?"

"It is, but there was an attack on the old location." Analise sounded exacerbated, worn out by the news. Mallor realized just how tiring her responsibilities were. He remembered the burden of leadership, reaching for her hand to comfort her.

"An attack?" He questioned her quietly, stroking her hand with his thumb.

"Hunters." She looked at him funny, tilting her head to the side.

"Why are you looking at me like that? I have no idea what you're talking about." Mallor put the pieces together, his eyes widening. "The hunters. I had no idea they were planning an attack on the location."

"An attack *on the location*? So you knew they were planning something in general?" She snatched her hand away from his.

"Analise, it's what hunters do. We exist to kill witches."

A scowl spread across her face. "*We?*" Anger crept into her voice. "You're not one of them, Mallor."

"Don't say that, Analise. You know I can't just let that part of me go." Mallor's tone grew tense, knowing it was reasonable to doubt his loyalty but feeling betrayed that she would after what they shared the night before.

"You're going to have to. I'm not taking you to the Election like that." She had shut down. Her voice was cold, and no ounce of affection remained.

"You're asking so much of me!" He sat up next to her, no longer wanting to be around her. "You did this to me, Analise."

"I did nothing to you. I have no idea when you're going to take responsibility for your actions, but it's about time you got with the program."

Mallor rolled his eyes. She was right, but he was not accepting defeat easily. "Can you just tell me when we need to go!" He got up out of bed, picking his clothes up off the floor. Sitting on the edge of the bed, he tied his shoes waiting for her answer.

The answer didn't come. Instead, the door of the bedroom slammed behind her as she left him alone in the room after their first night together. The air in the room became cold, and he sat there lonely wondering if the first bit of love he had found had disappeared in less than an hour.

CHAPTER 22

———

He sat there on the edge of the bed, unsure what to do. What did his father do when he argued with his mother? Did he do anything at all?

He realized the answer was no. His father always sat there, complacent, leaving his mother to ice her wounds alone. He realized he didn't want Analise to feel that way about him. He needed to get better, and although Mallor had no picture of what love looked like, he was determined to give this a shot.

If anything, Analise deserved more as his friend. She had taken care of him, and while he hated to admit it, what he had become wasn't her fault. If anything, she made him better.

He opened the door, pausing slightly to check the mirror by the door before he left. Cursing to himself in frustration, he accepted the sight of his being and went out the door.

Unsure what was on the other side of the door, he was surprised when he saw a bright-white-and-blue kitchen. Analise was washing dishes and cooking up eggs on the stove. Food smelled amazing, and his stomach grumbled loudly.

"Looks like being stubborn doesn't keep you from being hungry." She didn't turn to look at him, and while she sounded like she was pouting, he knew what would make it better.

He walked up to her and wrapped his arms around her. He kissed her neck lightly, pulling all of her in. The plate in her hand fell into the sink, and she smiled. Kissing his arm, she turned around and smiled at him.

"Stop doing that. You know I'm mad." She giggled, blushing as she melted in front of him.

"Right." He kissed her, deepening it as he realized no one was to blame here. What had happened was pure chance, and he was thankful it brought him closer to her. He wasn't sure how to apologize. He would rather make it up to her, but he knew it was important to say something.

"I'm so—"

She cut him off. "Don't worry about it." She looked at him endearingly, her eyes soft and forgiving. "It's been a long morning."

It was what went unspoken between them that proved to him how lucky he had gotten. While all he wanted was to go back to bed and lay with her, he knew the world was just outside the door of this kitchen.

"Where are we?"

"Just upstairs of the shop." She continued to brew coffee, flipping the eggs on the stove after. It was hard not to be infatuated with her, in her grace and goofiness.

"Is this where we met?"

She turned around to face him and gave him a shy smile. "It's not the exact store." She began pouring the coffee into two light blue mugs. "I wanted something that felt like home, and although I knew what you wanted to do to my family and maybe even me, this store where we met felt like home."

It was sweet. He was melting at the gesture but struggled to find the words.

"I hope you don't find that...too odd."

"No. I love it." His words came out quick and certain. It felt like home to him, and while the gesture was a bit out of the ordinary, it fit them.

The coffee cups were set down with a clink on the kitchen island. She pulled up a seat, a tall, white chair, and set one out for him too. There they sat across from each other, and he wanted to laugh with no idea of how to cope with how normal things seemed. He had never had a picture of love in his life, and while he was just getting to know Analise, he knew love was the direction this was headed in. It scared him to his core, but in moments like this, just like the morning they spent together watching cartoons, he wanted to lean into normalcy. He wasn't sure how long it would all last, but the beauty of the moment shoved away any second thoughts he had about fighting against it all.

"So we should leave in about thirty minutes. We'll teleport to Iro together, staying on the fringes of the city. The fighting starts in about ten hours at midnight. That's when we mobilize the witches here."

"Sounds good." He reached over and rubbed her arm, hearing the nerves in her voice. "Where is 'here' anyway?"

"What do you mean?"

"Well, what do you call this coven you've built?"

"Oh." She sipped her coffee slowly, her brows furrowing. "I've never really thought of it." Analise shrugged her shoulders, cutting into her eggs. The cutlery clicked together, the metal making gentle noises to compliment the birds chirping just outside the window.

"Well, that's something we should think about then. If you're going to be all big and successful, which you will be."

She kept her head down, joy creeping up on her face. He knew he had said "we." He'd done it intentionally. He hadn't figured everything out yet, especially because hunting still called to his soul morally. But he knew this was something she needed him for.

"Let's get going." She sprung up from the table, rather begrudgingly putting dishes in the sink.

"Should we do those?" Mallor walked over to the sink, wondering who was going to do the dishes if they didn't.

"Don't worry about it. We can do them when we get back."

He stayed facing the sink, looking at the dirty dishes covered in runny yolk. The remaining coffee grinds in the cups signified this moment and while he didn't want to dwell on the it, he also knew the idea of returning was still in the air. He loved being with her, but seeing his clan was going to be hard for him. He needed to return to them, but he really didn't know how he was going to bring his heart to do it. For the first time he no longer felt like "mind over matter," a phrase so frequently preached to him and tossed around as the men faced obstacles, was something he could believe in. He would figure it out when he got there, he supposed.

He spun around, ready to switch the subject. "Let's hit the road then."

———

He felt like they were in a Harry Potter novel as Analise brought him in front of the fireplace in the living room. Harry had landed in Diagon Alley unintentionally, and Mallor felt just as lost.

Those books often felt like a fever dream, each book intriguing him as they sat hidden in the bathroom cover as his mother read them again and again on rotation. He picked them up occasionally, running to hide them under his covers in the middle of the night and returning them to her bathroom before she awoke in the morning. He only got to the third book before his father found him reading past his bedtime and yelled at him. He never told his father whose books they really were.

Barring the fact this place was massive and clearly somewhere Analise used to get away from her responsibilities, he was ready to get going. He still felt conflicted, but all this stillness in one place was making him antsy. Plus, he was ready to get his hunt on. While he might not know which witches he had killed and which he may have to abandon, it was in his nature to finish them. Ending the lines of all eight covens would feel exhilarating. He was itching for it, and it showed.

"Calm down! If you don't focus, you're not going to be able to get yourself to the right place! Remember you ended up here when you tried to run!" Analise's words came out between cackles as Mallor bounced up and down, feeling goofy.

"Well, it's not my fault you have me under the fireplace as if we were in the *Chamber of Secrets!*" They laughed together, knowing the joke was only funny to the two of them and in the context of paradise they had created with one another.

"Shut up already!" Still laughing in little bursts, unable to get her directions out, they both fell into a laughing fit yet again.

"Clearly it's difficult to teach a wizard what the hell they're doing! Or, consider this, maybe you're just a bad teacher," he teased her, keeping her laughing at the top of her lungs.

"Maybe you're just a bad student! I'm the one with a whole coven."

"And I was one of the best hunters in the world!"

"Was?"

He rolled his eyes at the statement as their laughter tapered off. He looked her dead in the eyes with a little smirk on his face, slowly leaning in. "Am." He placed a kiss on her lips, playing with her limits before he ended it. She continued to reach for him, pouting.

"Okay, okay, we're already behind! Stop making me laugh; we have to go." She recomposed herself. "Picture a light-blue room. There's a canopy bed with light-pink sheets."

"Okay. We'll get to the pink sheets in a second."

She rolled her eyes at his flirty insinuation.

"What's a canopy bed?" The word sounded familiar, but Mallor couldn't put his finger on what to visualize.

"You're such a boy! Here I thought you would at least *enjoy* the pink sheets with me." Her suggestive comment took him aback, but he was at no means opposed to it.

"Enjoy?" He lifted an eyebrow at her, pushing her buttons.

"That's not what I meant!" She laughed, lightly shoving him aside. He pulled her in, placing his head above hers, taking a mental picture. A warm silence fell over the two of them, monumentalizing the moment.

"A canopy bed has four posts." Her tone was soft as she answered his earlier question.

"Like those beds royalty sleep in?" He wasn't sure in what world that kind of bed would be one he slept in.

"Like the bed we will be sleeping in if you stop asking me questions, dumbo."

"Dumbo is an elephant." He murmured and chuckled. He knew humor was the only way he knew how to respond to her comment.

"I have no idea when you became such a jokester, but we're going to have to speed this up."

"Okay, okay. Anything else distinctive in the room I should picture?"

"The floors are dark hardwood, similar to the ones in headquarters here." She pondered for a bit longer, furrowing her brows again in a way he was starting to find unbelievably cute. "Oh! Your wand will be sitting on the dark-brown, wooden nightstand."

"Are people already there?" He hated to admit it, but the idea of seeing some of the kinder witches he had gotten to know excited him.

"Lilith brought our stuff over last night as soon as they announced the location change."

Mallor made a sour face at the mention of Lilith's name. His excitement disappeared, knowing she was the last witch he wanted to see. She probably wouldn't be all that thrilled to see him either.

"Oh hush. She's lovely once you know her."

"Say that to the scars all over my back, Analise." He shuddered at the thought.

"I'm sorry. I'll kiss them better if that'll help?" She sounded genuine, and although her suggestion was cheesy, he was eager to oblige.

"I guess I can live with that."

She giggled at his response.

He shut his eyes abruptly, ready to teleport.

"Wait! Kiss goodbye!" She quickly leaned over when his eyes were still shut, and he swooned. He was convinced kissing her would never get old. Even just being around her could never get old.

"I'll see you there soon!" He opened his eyes and took one last look at her.

And just like that, she shut her eyes and disappeared.

Standing there alone in the room, he wondered what moment brought her hope. He wondered if it was the same moment he would think of. For once in his life, there were so many happy moments he wasn't even sure which to latch onto.

Squeezing his eyes shut once again, he let his thoughts flow before he fixated on one. He remembered waking up to her this morning, seeing her with her hair messily spread across the pillow and mouth open, breathing deep through her sleep, knowing he was looking at a version of her she would never let anyone else see. More mornings like that one were what brought him hope.

He pictured the room she had described, eager to get back into that bed with her.

The chirping birds around him disappeared and he knew he was on his way.

CHAPTER 23

——

"Ow! Mallor, move!" Analise groaned and tugged her arm out from under him.

Realizing he had accidentally landed on her, he rolled off and stood up. He wasn't sure when he would learn to land on his feet, but it was going to have to be soon. At some point, he would end up seriously injured. Or, as he was learning now, he would seriously injure someone else.

He checked to make sure they were in the room she had told him to picture. He smiled at the canopy bed across from him.

"Are you okay?" He was nursing a bruise on his side but knew he needed to check on her first. Without functioning arms, she couldn't perform magic.

"Yes, yes. Just a little scratch." Neither of them had stood up. They both just stayed there, laying on the floor together, knowing the second they stood up and started the day would be the moment everything changed. "We're going to have to teach you to land properly."

"Hey, at least be proud of the fact I got here!" Mallor's tone clearly encouraged banter. He mumbled, "Last time I couldn't even do that."

"I won't even ask where you were trying to go." He heard the lack of joy in the tone of her voice. Clearly she was still wounded from his attempt to run away. He understood why, and he had no idea how he could make it up to her.

"I'm sorry, Analise." He looked at her, propping his arm up through his elbow on the hardwood floor. "I'm just happy you found me."

"Of course I did." She shuffled up, finished with the discussion. He followed her lead, realizing now was not the time to be messing with her.

"So what's the plan?" Mallor felt a bit sheepish for asking, but the reality was they were no longer at the original location. Everything told to him the night before—a few nights before—may no longer apply. Unless the makeup of the covens were exactly the same, there was no chance every calculated step they discussed would still work.

"You'd think you'd never listened to Lina in your life." Analise sounded exasperated, and although she was clearly joking, there was a bit of her tone that worried Mallor. She was fed up with him. Less than three days ago, her anger would've caused him to doubt his own plan. Now, he just wanted to make sure they were okay.

"I listen to Lina! Lilith is the one I have a problem with." He clearly wanted to be here, and every moment he spent without making a decision made him feel like the weight of the world was getting heavier and heavier. His original goal of exterminating the witches wouldn't work anymore. It *couldn't* work anymore. He wasn't sure he could look Analise in the eye—or let anyone else look her in the eye—and kill her. This meant only the main eight would go. This would leave Analise's coven, which Mallor was now part of.

We. He was beating himself up in his head for telling her he would name the coven with her. He didn't know where he would be. He had grown up lying and breaking promises, but it was getting harder and harder to lie. Maybe it was a witch thing. Ugh, he hadn't even figured out how or if he was going to tell the men he was a wizard. This constant internal conflict was getting really annoying, and he just wished someone would tell him what to do.

Seemingly in direct response to his wishes, Analise laid out a map. She set it on the bed that Mallor hadn't even noticed in the emotional turmoil of her constantly switching attitude. The map looked familiar, and Mallor realized he had seen it prior because he had drawn it up before his mission to Iro with Cell. It was the old map he carried around with him but had lost on a mission.

"Where did you get that?" His thoughts reeled. He never realized it had been stolen.

"Where we get all of our maps from. The hunters."

"How could you possibly have access to them?"

"Remember how I told you Lilith was able to track your actions?" While it was a question, she stated it as if it were an explanation. Maybe Mallor was getting dumber, or just showcasing how bad at school he used to be, but he wasn't putting the pieces together.

"She would need a piece of the hunters. Finding a piece of every hunter that went on a mission to anywhere new? That sounds damn near impossible to track."

"When are you going to realize the witches have been planning to get what we need from hunters *for hundreds of years.* We've figured how to use you all to our advantage if you couldn't tell." She brushed off his question, returning to the task at hand without care.

"Ouch." He was already upset to hear they had hunter maps, but the feeling was worsened when she acted like it didn't matter.

"Please, Mallor, don't act like you would've wanted it any other way." She insinuated yet again he wanted to be a wizard, forgetting he was set up.

"I didn't want it this way, even if I had thought about wanting you." He was growing tired of having the same conversation again and again.

"You couldn't have both." She was stern in her words.

"I know that. That's why I'm here, Analise." For once, he appreciated her bluntness. It was true.

She looked at him, processing what he had just said. It was as if she thought he was here for the cause. Mallor realized she had never considered he wouldn't be here for a witch cause. It was her from the second they met. She continued to look at him with confusion sprawled across her face. He let her confusion linger.

"So are you going to explain how you have this map?"

"Remember those witches who attacked your coven before Leon's?" She straightened out the parchment, trying to rid it of wrinkles.

"They were yours? We thought they were from Iro."

"They're told to act like they're from different clans. That's the role they serve in every fight." She said it as if it were a matter of fact.

"But why would they try to kill us?"

"They came for a piece of your hair. But, realistically, the more hunters we kill, the better it is for us."

Mallor felt disgust spread across his face.

"Oh, please, Mallor. Don't tell me you haven't thought about how to kill every witch you've come across both here and before."

Mallor shrugged, defeated by her accurate accusation. "Well obviously. It's what I've been trained to do! You can't ask me to go against my basic human nature."

"That's not human nature. You're just as much a killer as we are." She shrugged her shoulders at the harsh reality she was telling him about. "You do this because you have been raised to. We kill to survive."

"Surviving would have been to stay human."

"It isn't that easy! You have no idea why I'm here."

"Power, Analise. The whole reason any of you witches continued the tradition of changing from human women to witches was for power."

"We're not all like that." Her voice grew shaky. She turned her back to him, hands shaking as she traced over the map mindlessly. She was defensive, as if he were fighting her and not a here to fight *for* her.

"You can't tell me your change wasn't intentional."

"Of course it wasn't! I was forced to turn, Mallor!" A tear ran down her face.

He was infuriated. Someone had forced her to become this way. It had never occurred to him that forceful changing was possible. "What happened, Analise?"

"Senali isn't just my sister by coven. She's my natural born sister."

This was news to Mallor. He had constant news from the magical world, so he was sure very few knew this happened. It was also often tradition for biological siblings to split up and go to different covens. Siblings were so different it was rare they chose to stick together after choosing to change.

"Senali had grown up admiring the witches." Analise sniffled, continuing as pain strained her voice. "She hated herself every second she spent with humans. As her younger sister,

I saw that and wondered what was wrong with me. I never wanted to change, though. We had a really happy family."

She took a deep breath.

"She saw me pick up on her hatred. She saw I wanted to be like her. I always bought the same books. Everything she had, I wanted in the same color. Where she went, I went. She pulled my sisters and I aside one night and told us she knew how to make us better. She told us we were going to change and a witch, Helena, would take care of us."

"What about your mother?" Mallor was eager to ask questions.

"Mallor, if I don't get through this story in one shot, I may never tell you again."

"Sorry."

She continued on, her sadness shifting to anger as the story got more concerning. "There were five of us. Helena, myself, two sisters, and one younger brother. I refused to go without every one of us." She put her hand over her mouth, holding back tears.

"We took my younger brother to kill with us. Helena wanted *us*, and although I think we both knew it wouldn't work to turn him, we had convinced ourselves it would work."

She stopped talking. Silence continued for minutes, and although Mallor didn't want to press, he needed her to tell him. He couldn't be there for her without understanding the full extent of the story.

"Did it?" His question was spoken quietly, almost hoping she wouldn't hear him. He feared the answer.

"No." She began sobbing. "It didn't work. Helena changed and Noah tried. Noah died within a few hours, and the two youngest refused to change."

"Holy shit, Analise. That's heavy."

"We never saw my youngest sisters again. I'm not sure what happened, because Helena tells me they ran, but I saw the anger in her eyes when they refused to give into her plan. She was fuming and was ready to kill them. Her first kill made her lethal, and she's only gotten worse since."

"I was forced to turn, Mallor. The anger in Helena's eyes, looking like she was going to kill my youngest sister just after Noah died? I had to change for the youngest girls to run. I hope they got far enough, but as soon as I took my first bite of my first kill, I blacked out. They had to have run as soon as I started the kill process, because Helena would have surely caught them otherwise." Her hiccups from quiet sobs had slowed down. She wiped her tears, sat up straighter, and her voice came out sternly.

"You have no idea what many of these witches have been through. And until you realize their story is the same as yours, you'll never be able to fight with focus. You were a boy from a poor family given up so your parents could give you power and gain some for themselves. A lot of us used magic to escape our pain. I do believe there are some corrupt witches, and through killing the eight covens, we can exterminate them. But from then on, I want my connection to the human world back. It is what Noah would've wanted."

Analise gave him no time to answer her before she began rambling about the plans for the day. She etched signs and strategy into the massive map, and although he watched her hand move across the page in grace, he was lost in the story she told him. Had everything he had been taught about witches been wrong?

CHAPTER 24

Iro looked beautiful from his window. He would never get used to the lethalness of the coven and knowing how many innocent people had been lured in and died, but he could appreciate it for what it was. The architecture was modern, and the coven looked nothing like the others he had seen. It was covered in green, the buildings growing beautiful vines of leaves through them. The buildings were black and white and the colors glistening as if the paint were redone each day. It was all intentionally set up, but in a way it looked natural. It put you at ease, and part of him wondered if the calmness of the plants was to mask the death that occurred in and around the coven every single day.

Analise had left to run over the plan a final time with the court. She was dressed in a stunning deep red when she left, not trying to be undercover at all. He had assumed they would be hiding until they fought, but it was only him and Analise's witch court that were hiding.

Analise would tell the covens fighting in the Election that night she was back. Well, she didn't intend to *tell* them. She intended to show up to what they called "the final dinner," where each witch knew only one of them would be living the night after. He didn't know how Analise managed to make this happen, but he guessed she had someone working for her on the inside.

For now, Mallor was just waiting. They would storm the Election after Analise had killed the eight witches fighting, including her sister because Helena had replaced Analise.

The plan sounded an awful lot like the one he made with the hunters, which struck him as very ironic. He wanted to protest her plan, knowing it sounded like one that was made for a band of humans. But he also knew this is what Cell thought would work, so it would.

In the silence, as he sat sipping a cup of ginger lemon tea by the white dining table in the little house they had ended up at, he pondered his hunters. He wondered if they were there, but he had seen no indication they were. He hoped they hadn't gotten lost, but he had also hoped they *had*. He still didn't know what decision to make, and the conversation he just had with Analise didn't make his conflict any easier.

The noise in his head was so loud. He wished for just a minute he could turn it off. He wished so greatly he could enjoy this love he had found and fallen into. He sat there, flipping through the stack of books. His eyes glossed over the pages, trying to give the books the attention they deserved. He was never a big reader, and while he was a quiet personality, generally in school he always tried to be a class clown in English class. He knew the more he chatted with Ms. Laurenti, the less work the class would have to do. He liked her too, and part of him always had a puppy crush on her.

He smiled to himself, reminiscing on days that were once so simple. Oh, how odd life seemed now. He daydreamed, recollecting all the best days of his youth. He remembered the times he biked across the block with his friends and played soccer on the fields in the sun. He wished he could be young again. He never thought he would miss those days, knowing most of them ended in physical and emotional hurt, but a part of him felt like they were simple. At least he always knew what was coming back then.

Now he felt like he knew nothing.

As if on cue, he heard a familiar voice from outside his window. He was on the second floor of their house, but the windows were all open to give him some fresh air. The gruff voice he grew up with was monopolizing the conversation. Cell.

Cell was telling someone what the plan was. Mallor froze, adrenaline kicking in as he sought to make out the words. Cell was too far away, and Mallor was ready to punch a wall. He knew it was Cell. It had to be. Did he really know? Maybe he was just imagining things.

He needed to check. If he knew, he would feel safe again. Part of him hoped seeing a familiar face would remind him of the decision he knew was right to make.

He got out of his chair and crouched, crawling to the window. He didn't want the men to see him. They would wonder why he was here, and he wasn't sure he had an explanation. He could just say he caught up with them and was waiting, but that would mean once the lie was told and he was covering up who he had really become, he could never go back.

He was nearing the window when the voices got louder. Feeling like a puppy looking out the window for their owner, he peeked his head up and looked down.

It was Cell. He seemed to be speaking to a trainee, as the boy looked young and rather lanky to be of higher accord. Mallor's mind went blank.

He kept an ear open to listen and watched as Cell did what he did best: give orders. The familiar voice gave him ease, but also caused his mind to go blank. He couldn't tear his eyes away, even though he knew the longer he looked, the more likely he was to get caught. He was laying eyes on family. He knew it.

But if he knew it, why did this feel so wrong?

The talking stopped and a silence had never felt so loud. They were looking at a map, which Mallor recognized as one very similar to what Analise had shown him earlier that day.

With no warning or tell, Cell looked up directly at Mallor. They caught eyes quickly, and Mallor shot back down into a crouched position. He flipped his back to the wall beneath the windowsill, hoping no one had seen him. He would just have to hope Cell had forgotten what Mallor's eyes looked like. Just minutes ago he was praying it was Cell to feel safe. So why, all of a sudden, was he praying the hunters were nowhere near?

CHAPTER 25

Analise and Mallor were laying on the couch together. Analise returned around 11 p.m. to find him pacing around their room. He didn't know how to explain to her his distress without sounding like he had been looking for the hunters.

"I'm just worried about the fight. It's okay." He had told her a partial truth, reaching for her hand and taking a seat next to her.

The fighting would begin at 1:30 a.m., after the ceremonial prayer that would connect the covens together. Holding each other tight, they didn't bother to speak further about the plans for the night.

He knew the hunters were planning for this, for the chance to end each coven by killing all eight of the witches. He also knew the hunters did not know Helena's death wouldn't bring the death of Cinder. Analise had to be killed for everyone to die. He wasn't sure what to do with this information, but he knew he wanted her to live.

He remembered how young they both were by looking at her dress. The beautiful, red ballgown glittered even after her long night, and she was a sight for sore eyes wearing a dress instead of the business clothes she felt obligated to don.

She was jittery, unable to fall asleep at a regular time due to the lateness of the fight. Most would nap, but she had told him naps made her head hurt and merely disoriented her. Plus, they had spent most of the night before in bed. It was unusual for both of them, this level of rest.

Here they were, two teenagers head over heels for one another with no idea of what would happen next. They knew Analise could die that night, and this thought gave everything a sense of urgency. Even if she won the Election and went through Metamorphosis, the rumors of the pain sat with him. He had once told the men there was no way Cinder would let her fight because she would die. And now she was choosing to fight on her own, he felt no better about her chances of living through it.

"Are you okay?" Mallor couldn't help feeling her grip on his arm tighten over the night. While she had started comfortably, he could see her thoughts eating her alive. He wasn't sure how to help her and was starting to believe that there was really nothing he could do.

"Honestly?" She looked at him, eyes big.

He nodded, knowing he meant his question but also knowing he was also not okay. *How are we supposed to do this?*

"I'm scared, Mallor." She looked away as if embarrassed to admit this.

He stroked her hair, holding her closer. Both of their grips tightened, as if the world depended on how close they were to each other.

"Let's go for a walk." Her suggestion came out of nowhere but sounded more like a need than a want. She was urgent, and he understood the need to move to make things feel okay.

"Won't we get caught?" His question was valid, but at this he wanted to get out as much as he did. He felt like movement was the only thing that would soothe his worries.

"Every family is getting their chosen witch ready for the fight. They all have their own rituals. I actually forgot about them in all this planning, which means we're just riding the waiting wave."

"I wouldn't blame yourself for having forgotten something." He kissed her forehead. "You've planned this far."

"Can we please go for a walk?" Nothing he said would get past her need to move.

"Of course. Should we change into something less noticeable?"

She sprung up, flipping open the suitcases Lilith had packed and brought for them with Lina. "Yes. Throw this on."

She chucked a black pair of pants and sweatshirt at him. She threw on a very similar outfit, and no matter how quickly she was moving, he couldn't help but take a minute and admire her. Every curve of her body was beautiful, and if he had his choice, he would repeat what they had done just last night.

He craved closeness with her in any capacity.

"Hey, mister, stop looking at me like that." She stuck her tongue out, making a goofy face.

"No matter what you do, you couldn't stop me from looking at you like that."

He wanted so badly to tell her about the day he had. *I saw Cell. I saw him. My old family.*

But he also knew he couldn't. She was in no place to process this information because even he was barely in the right headspace.

She melted in front of him, her eyes going soft. Only half-dressed, she walked over to him and placed a kiss on his cheek. He tried to kiss her on the lips, but she smiled and playfully pushed him onto the bed. "Get dressed; we've got a walk to go on and not long enough for you to distract me."

"So you're saying I distract you?" he teased her, but felt a bit of honest wonder seep through. For a woman like her to feel like he was a distraction blew his mind. How lucky he had gotten.

He finally threw on his sweatshirt, grabbed her by the hand, and set stride out the door.

If we see them, I'll tell her.

CHAPTER 26

———

The gust of cold hit him sharply. He realized it had been quite a while since he had walked outside freely, not running from or to something. The relief was jolting, and even a bit uncomfortable. A part of his mind would always be on high alert. There was no way around it. He was wired to be on edge, and he knew it impacted his listening skills.

"Mallor! Hello?" Analise waved a hand in front of his face to get his attention. "Have you even been listening?"

"Sorry. I was just...making sure there was no one around." He was picking at the skin around his fingernails, unable to process the freedom this night was affording him.

"If you had listened to me, you would've heard me tell you where everyone is!"

"Okay, I'm sorry." He was a bit fed up with her tone, given he was just trying to protect her from the eyes of the hunters. "What were you saying?" He rolled his eyes, but when he looked at her, he realized he was being unreasonable. She had no idea the hunters were here. In some way, Mallor wanted to convince himself he didn't know they were there. Nothing could deny Cell's voice, however. Mallor knew it too well, and holding this secret from Analise was hurting him. He knew it was for the best. At least, for now.

He squeezed her hand to show her he was listening, and in some ways, it was him committing to the apology he had so quickly said out of irritation. She squeezed his hand back, and just like that, he knew they were fine. He would never get used to the healthy resolving of conflict as he was so used to seeing any argument in the context of love end in a physical fight.

"I was saying how nice it is to have some quiet." She looked up at the sky, continuing to walk forward. He couldn't help but smile at her, continuously floored by how blissfully she walked the earth despite the hurt she had been put through. Her resilience was beyond him. Through everything she had been put through, she still sought to connect the human and magical worlds, likely at her own expense. She gave up her family and every bit of safety she had to do a good thing. There was very little doubt about her winning the Election, and she had given up the chance for power and status all to do what she thought was right. It was hard to remember she was a witch, especially when he classified all witches as downright selfish and evil. "Everyone is getting ready, and no one would dare leave their homes."

"Why is that? Wouldn't they want to flaunt their power?"

"No. If you leave your house as one of the witches fighting, or a witch in association, you could be killed by an enemy coven. Realistically, everyone is looking to dwindle the competition before the fight even starts."

This statement put fear in Mallor's heart. "Then why the hell are we out here?" He wasn't sure if she was being intentionally stupid, but what she said meant they had to be alert for danger from every angle. In a second she could be killed, and he wasn't powerful enough to help her if it were against a group of witches. He wasn't emotionally prepared to fight his own clan for her. Succinctly put, Mallor realized just how useless he was to her.

"Relax! No one is coming out here tonight. The eight families have signed a contract. If anyone is killed before the Election starts, the Election is postponed another year." She chuckled to herself. "The fights the night before the Election were a shit-show when electing the first Original Witch. She damn near won by default, given only three of the witches survived to even show up to the fight."

Mallor remembered learning about that in history. Apparently, when the first Original Witch won, there were only five covens. Two of the witches chosen to fight among the five were killed. This was actually how the hunters figured out the witch lines would all die off if they were all connected after the ceremony. Everyone had to be killed while they were connected, but hunters were rare back then. The Original Witch obviously survived the Election, meaning the lines did not die out. Had someone killed her, the entirety of magic would cease to exist for long enough to keep any other women from turning through policy.

Still, something wasn't sitting well with Mallor. "Isn't that a good thing? Wouldn't you all want extra time?" Mallor was sure pushing the Election by one year would mean the witches could train better.

"No. It gives more time for the remaining witches to be killed. Each coven would be left with so few witches to fight, and the whole year would be war. Everyone wants the power that comes with being the second Original Witch, but not enough to damn the witching community."

He nodded, taking in the new information.

"It's tonight or never, Mallor. The Election has to go on." Analise's voice went cold, and the determination in her voice was enough to make anyone believe she could change the world.

The two continued to walk, and Mallor realized he had to let his guard down before Analise kept wondering why he was zoning out. It was making him cranky, the idea this might be his last night with her and he couldn't even enjoy it in peace. Frankly, the hunters had no reason to be out this early. The plan was for them to station themselves mid-Election when a few witches had already been killed. The goal was to kill the winner and finally end every line. The witches in each eight lines would die out, but again, Helena was not the Cinder witch. It was Analise, and no one knew she was still connected to them.

Only a few seconds after he had finally relaxed his shoulders and unclenched his jaw did he go back on high alert. In front of him was a store filled with blood. And, my god, did it smell good.

He never understood why Iro was where some witches settled. They could have the same privileges everywhere else, and all the history books attributed it to the blood. The descriptions were vivid. Using words like *delectable, smooth,* and *perfectly aged,* Mallor had always scoffed at the way witches made blood sound like wine.

The descriptions now made complete sense. The mere scent was intoxicating. He couldn't imagine what it would *taste* like. Analise was mid-sentence, and he heard her stop speaking when she noticed him drifting away. He felt physically compelled to go near the blood, trying to justify it by reasoning it would fuel his magic. His mind was going blank, and he found himself unable to argue with the fact every ounce of his being *wanted the blood.*

"We can go in if you want." Analise seemed not to understand the conflict going on his mind.

"What? No. I can't." The scent was pulling at him, a seductive force he wouldn't be able to stop unless he stood his ground.

"Yes, you can. It's still open." She pointed to the flashing *OPEN* sign on the storefront.

She wasn't looking at him but was walking in front of him toward the store. She placed her hand on the metal handle and stopped when he spoke. "No, Analise. You know I can't do that."

"What?" She furrowed her brow, taking a step back from him.

"I can't drink blood, Analise." He had hoped his voice would come out stern, but inside it was quiet and timid.

"Mallor, stop denying what you are!" She stepped back toward him fervently.

"Stop it, Analise." He was getting frustrated, trying to hush her into being quiet so no one would hear her.

"I wish you would just stop trying to fight the fact you're not a hunter anymore!"

"Why would I do that? Of course, I'm still a hunter!" He was getting paranoid and cornered the two of them into the alley by the store. His voice came out as a whisper, but it was clear he was yelling.

"Stop whispering! You've eaten someone. Less than twenty-four hours ago, I found you in a blood store!"

"Why are you so insistent on me being proud of this? There is nothing to be proud of. No matter how much power I have now and no matter how many tricks you teach me, I will never be proud of what I am."

Her eyes began to well up, and Mallor was beyond confused as to why she was the one crying. If anything, he felt like bursting out into tears.

"So you'll never be proud of me. Fair enough. I should've known." Her voice came out as a squeak. She wiped her tears, and while he tried to put his hand on her arm and tell her it wasn't true, she pushed him away and walked to the store. She swung the door open and slammed it. He was left in the cold with no hand to hold and a desire to drink everything in front of him.

———

It took Mallor far too long to come to his senses. Standing there, pitying himself, he realized he needed her support.

He quickly headed toward the door, knowing she was eating inside. He swung the door open and looked at her sitting on the floor with a blood bag in her hands. She sucked the blood through a straw, and as queasy as it made him, it also made him salivate to see someone drinking blood so freely.

"Please leave, Mallor. You've made yourself very clear." Her voice shook, and he realized just how badly he hurt her. He had no idea how to get her to trust he did support her. It was more than supporting the mission, it was supporting her in every way she tried to make the world better. She was selfless and had been since that night her brother was killed. He was selfish, feeling sorry for himself when she had been through so much worse.

He did the only thing he knew how to do. He grabbed a blood bag from the glass case on the wall, fiddling with the handle for a minute. Popping a straw into it, he plopped down on the floor next to her. He looked her in the eyes and began to sip.

In grade school, he expected blood to taste like metal. It always tasted a bit like copper when he got a cut on his finger helping his mom chop veggies or when he sliced himself on his homework. But this was sweet. It tasted of honey and syrup and went down smoothly with the thickness of cream. It was *addicting*.

The action physically hurt. He knew it was wrong, but it felt insanely good. He felt recharged, as if he had slept for days. His mind was hit with a wave of clarity, and although he was in no space to use it now, he was grateful for the relief the blood provided. He shut his eyes, embracing the full experience of what was happening. At this rate, he would move to Iro.

Suddenly, Analise's lips were on his. Both of them tasting a bit of blood, they smiled at each other and leaned into the kiss. She put her hand on the back of his neck, pulling him toward her. Laying on the floor, embracing being together in the way that was most natural, Mallor pushed away the feeling they were being watched.

CHAPTER 27

───

A warm shower served them both nicely. Analise had just left him for the opening ceremony and prayer, and he could feel her last kiss to him lingering on his lips. The night had been pleasant, and he was sure it would forever be one of his favorite memories. He had forgotten any fear or paranoia that had accompanied him through their walk and chose to place that memory away as a good one. He had too many memories that had been corrupted by fear, and he was tired of feeling like loss would follow every great moment of his.

Now, he was just waiting. He sat at the dinner table with a cup of tea Analise made him when she saw him bouncing his knee. "I'll see you soon," she said, hugging him from behind. She said it with such conviction, and he couldn't imagine it not being true. She had a way of doing that, making everything feel real.

The time was passing, and he could hear the ticking of the clock above the kitchen cabinets click away. With every second, he kept pushing himself to make a decision. He loved her, he knew that. Whether it was young love or too fast, he didn't care. It was what it was, and he chose to accept it. However, he still wasn't sure if that was enough. He believed in her cause, but taking the side of witches was a whole other story. It was in his nature to kill the witches, and although he was in love with one, it didn't change the fact staying here with her would mean keeping many of them alive.

His mind went numb like dull static, exhausted by the prospect of having to decide within the hour. It would be midnight soon, and he would have to leave for the Election. He didn't know whose side he would be on. Worse, he was starting to wonder if the side he *should* be on was different from the one he *wanted* to be on.

The clock ticked away, and it felt like the sound of the hands moving was only getting louder. He hummed to himself, not able to put his finger on the song he chose but making it up as he went. He laughed at himself and his situation, realizing just how crazy everything had gotten in a matter of weeks.

He decided he might as well watch some TV, hoping somehow an answer for his dilemma would come to him.

As he stood up, a rock broke through the window. He ducked, instinct kicking in despite him being far back enough from the window to not have gotten in. Attached to the rock was a piece of string, a small piece of paper dangling from it. Mallor crawled to the note through glass from the broken window, eager to ensure no one from outside the window could see him.

His stomach dropped the whole way. He knew who it was from, and despite wishing he could ignore it, the messy handwriting sprawling on the piece of paper made it very clear Cell had sent this his way. Cell had seen him today. Mallor had known this for the last few hours, but somehow he just kept hoping it was in his mind. He hoped he was going crazy and making people up. Needing to be hospitalized for hallucinations felt better than dealing with his reality.

The clock continued to tick, and Mallor read the note.

Hey man.

I'm not sure if this is going to you given I only caught a brief glimpse of you before you ducked away like a coward. I'm pretty sure it was you, and if this isn't Mallor then please chuck this away. If you're still reading and your name isn't Mallor, then I have no idea why you are in Iro as a man. You're probably a coward too.

If this is Mallor, I just wanted to say hi. We miss you, dude. I'll kill you if you ever tell the clan that. Speaking of the clan, are you coming back? We're here on the original plan. We didn't know where you had gone, and a part of me was convinced you were here because you caught up to us. I had no idea how you survived, but then I saw you today with Analise.

In that little store on the corner. Were you drinking blood? What have you become?

And then you kissed her! Was that Analise? Shouldn't she be in the Cinder house? Or are the rumors about her sister replacing her true?

The point is, I'm not here to shame you. I'll do tons of that later.

We need you, Mallor. The boys are a mess, and everything has been tumultuous since we lost you. I nearly killed Leon for losing you, even though it wasn't really his fault. Did you leave to find Teil? Did you forget what the Cinder witches did to Teil?

You can answer these questions when you come back. The point is you must come back. Normally I'd think about playing you or tricking you to come back here. But I know I saw a man in love in that store. We'll keep Analise alive. After all, if Helena is fighting in her place, then we have no need to kill Analise. Granted, she's a disgusting witch, but we'll get to that later. Come fight with us. Help us end the lines. You can keep her. I'm not sure what your plan is now, and I hope this isn't that different from what it was. If you kissed her because you intend to kill her, we'll jump on board with that too.

We just want you back here. Meet me at the store where you were with Analise right before the Election begins. You can catch up on the stakeout plan and we'll use the plan the two of us came up with months ago to end this once and for all. Don't be late, Mallor.

-C

And just like that, the note ended. Mallor knew Cell was an expert strategist, but it blew his mind he was willing to compromise like this for him. Normally, Cell would rather end his own life than spare a witch's life. He wasn't sure what changed, but Cell made it sound like the clan needed him. Mallor understood the desperation. For months after Teil had been pronounced dead, he felt the absence of a leader on every mission. He took that pain and filled the hole in the clan's leadership, but he didn't realize he was this indispensable. Cell was rarely emotional. This was about the softest he got, and even with that, Mallor felt the anger in Cell's words.

The proposed plan, however, was ideal. Cell knew he was here. He didn't know what Mallor was, even if he speculated a bit. Analise got to live. Screw the other witches.

He began packing his bag, changing into the clothing he would need for a long night of massacre.

The clock ticked away, and for once, he felt like time was moving toward something with clarity.

A bounce in his step had returned, and it was apparent. He couldn't believe he had gotten so lucky. He didn't have to compromise his moral compass, and there was a way for him to protect Analise. He knew this was Cell's strategy to achieve his own life-long goal: to kill the witches. Cell, just like Mallor, was intent on ruining them all. Neither of them wanted them to exist, and Mallor had spent so long feeling ashamed of ending the lines after meeting the witches over this last week. His mind had swayed a bit, but something in his gut told him he was doing the right thing.

Packing his belongings didn't take very long. For once in his life, he had items he didn't want to leave behind. So much of the clothing Analise had picked out for him, among the other accessories he valued with love, were things he cherished. He also knew he could come back for them. Right now, his main mission was following Cell's direction of "*don't be late.*"

The words pushed him to move faster, as if it were even possible. While his original armor for the Election fight was built by Lina and Analise's coven, it was far too flashy for him to take. It was pure metal, and much of it glistened like a mirror. He looked like a tin man in it, and when he had tried it on for Analise, she giggled. The moment stuck with him, her setting aside how he looked and reminding him the armor would be integral to his safety. It was sweet how she worried, and while he desperately wanted to take the articles of clothing with him, it wouldn't be possible. He needed to get out the door quickly, and he was itching to see the men again.

However, the trek back to the store would require the utmost inconspicuousness. If he was caught and Analise found out he left, he would have no way to tell her of the plan. He considered sending her a message, finding a way to clarify he would be gone. Although he had a phone and had quickly typed out the text, he thought about her phone going off during the open ceremony and decided against sending it. He was also worried someone else would intercept it, and he couldn't count on Lina or Lilith to be the ones to see it. If someone else found out he was there and the message landed in the wrong hands, he was screwed.

In some ways, it was better she didn't know. He wasn't sure if she'd understand, and she would surely see it as betrayal. Her goal wasn't mass murder, and while he had never been ashamed this was his goal, he was ashamed to admit it to her.

He threw on the same sweatshirt and training pants as earlier, laced up his shoes, and adjusted the bit of protective gear he had under the sweatshirt. He was able to wear a bit of it given it didn't inhibit his mobility. He quickly ran to the bathroom, looking at himself in the mirror.

He took a deep breath in and reassured himself he could do this. He could have everything he had ever wanted and damn anyone who told him otherwise.

One foot in front of the next, he was out the door within minutes. His wand strapped to the inside of his sleeve to hide from the men, his being buzzing to do what he knew best, he quietly shut the door behind him.

CHAPTER 28

———

Seeing Cell's silhouette felt like finding the light at the end of a very dark tunnel. He was unmistakably himself, a small knife creating an indent in the back of his shirt where it laid under the fabric. Seeing a knife excited Mallor. The weapons in Cell's world were familiar to Mallor. They reminded him although his magic was his secret weapon, there was nothing like the knives he had been trained to use for years.

Cell was averse to physical affection. Rarely one to even shake someone's hand out of respect, he hated being touched. It set him off. But as he turned around hearing Mallor's footsteps quickening, Cell launched himself at him in a hug.

The affectionate embrace nearly knocked the air out of Mallor, not to mention made the wand tucked so carefully into his sleeve nearly fall out. He returned the hug with surprise, gleefully patting Cell. This was the love he wasn't used to, but the presence of this man who had been his partner through so much felt right.

"Good to see you, man!" Childlike excitement filled Cell's voice. He was beaming, all emotions on display. It was uncommon to see him like this, and Mallor took a mental picture to remember every bit of his expression. If anything, he would make fun of Cell tomorrow when this was all over for abandoning his poker face.

"Feels great to be back with you, Cell." Mallor's voice was enveloped by the smile that sprawled across his face. He realized why Cell couldn't keep his emotions to himself. The two men had so little practice hiding joy. They were used to hiding fear and anxiety, and in this moment they seized the rush of happiness.

"What the hell happened to you!" Chuckling, he playfully punched Mallor's arm. The question took him aback, but he decided to say what he had rehearsed on the way.

"I got lost when I went on a walk from Leon's." He took a breath in. "I was mortified I would never find my way back, and it seemed like the woods I had gotten lost in were fully deserted." His voice wavered on the latter statement. It was true. He had been mortified. Until this moment, that unexplainable fear had not left him. For just one moment, he had ease here with Cell. He felt relieved.

"That's what we thought! I figured you'd find us soon enough." Cell didn't stop smiling for even a second. He cleared his throat. "But what's with Analise?"

Mallor knew exactly what to say. "She found me in the woods. Guess she just couldn't resist this." He gestured up and down his body, laughing. He had run through trillions of explanations regarding Analise but hoped a boyish explanation would work.

It did. Cell doubled over laughing at Mallor's goofiness, hitting him in the arm and rolling his eyes.

"Fair enough, man. Guess you couldn't resist her even though she's a witch?" The playfulness in Cell's voice disappeared. His question wasn't accusatory, but it was skeptical.

"Guess love just is what it is. I never really understood it, but she's on our side. She's not a fan of the witches either."

Mallor knew this was only half of the truth, but he hoped it was enough he could get away with the white lies he was hiding. Cell raised his eyebrows, looking at Mallor as if he were an idiot. "Really?" Cell had laid the sarcasm on thick, but Mallor chose to ignore it.

"Yeah." He didn't feel like elaborating. He had promised himself he would only answer what was asked of him. It was the easiest way to make sure he didn't slip up. He was serious, and he knew the more he tried to defend her, the more Cell would stop trusting him.

"How can you trust her? They're all unworthy, Mallor." His voice grew cold, realizing just how serious Mallor was. Cell only knew what he was taught, and while just a week ago Mallor would've agreed, he knew now Cell only spoke out of ignorance.

"She was forced to turn. She wouldn't be this way if she could choose." Mallor knew this was a secret that wasn't his to share. In some ways, he felt dirty saying it, but it was the truth. He could lie about a lot but being forced to do something painful was something every hunter understood. Being given up by your family was rarely something you wanted, and Mallor prayed he would get the reference.

"Okay."

Cell's response confused Mallor. Had he just accepted that? "That's it?"

"Well, I don't agree with her kind, but if being her kind is something she doesn't want, we have something in common. I don't want her to be a witch either. We could at least find a way to use her as our secret weapon."

Mallor was stunned by the open mindedness Cell was showing. Some of it was shrouded in the idea they could take advantage of what Analise had to offer, but Mallor figured he would deal with that later. They were making progress.

"She stays alive then." This was the most important thing to him. Mallor refused to give up Analise no matter how much he wanted this.

"Those were the terms of our agreement. Ask me one more time and I might change my mind."

"Fair enough."

A small pause lingered in the air. The mix of emotions overwhelmed them both, and if they stood here forever, they wouldn't get to fight the battle they had been preparing their whole hunting careers for.

"Well, where are the boys?"

"Just up the hill. They're staking out for about fifteen more minutes." Cell spoke with excitement, as if he had waited his whole life to be asked this question. "The Election starts soon, and they'll shift into place midway through."

"Perfect."

They began walking up the hill, continuing to chat strategy like old times. Mallor had to keep his mind from wandering to excitement about how *correct* this all felt.

"Nothing's really changed then?" They were coming up on the men, and while Mallor couldn't hear them as they were surely staying quiet in hiding, he could sense them in a way only someone who led the hunt could. Cell had spent the ten-minute walk talking Mallor through the logistics of the night. Everything seemed just about the same, except Analise was no longer the Cinder target. Helena was.

Mallor knew Cinder wouldn't die if Helena was killed. He wasn't worried, however, as Analise mentioned they were creating a plan to ensure Helena would be tied to Cinder by the end of the night. He hadn't pressed the topic, knowing talking about killing her entire family would make her unstable on a night where she needed the most power she ever had.

"Nope. The original plan stands through, even if you're a little late to the event."

Mallor chuckled, loving every second of this time he had with Cell before the real hunt began.

And just like that, lost in laughter, Mallor saw the court tucked away on the top of the hill.

———

In whispers that felt louder than shouts, the men saw him and tackled him.

He was welcomed back home. The voices of Tate and Faidor blended with the excited murmurs of everyone. After each and every hug went around and the men beamed at his return, Mallor turned to Cell.

"You didn't tell them I was coming back?"

"Figured we all needed some good news and a surprise. I also didn't know if you'd fail me." Cell smirked at him, clearly knowing Mallor's return would bring the men exactly what they needed.

"Wouldn't dream of it." Mallor patted Cell's back, then turned toward the group who had gathered in front of him. "Alright boys, are we ready to go?"

Mallor knew he had to keep his voice down but coming back into his element as a leader felt like home in a way that put learning how to use magic for the first time to waste. The men all nodded aggressively, some whispering "hell yeah."

He had so many questions for them, eager to learn about how they knew the Election had moved and how they'd gotten here in time. Teleportation was one thing but doing this by foot was a feat. He was proud of them, and although he would rarely articulate that directly, he hoped they could see it in his eyes.

He was home.

CHAPTER 29

———

The hunt was beginning.

Everyone eager to chat, Cell quickly shut them down and reminded them that, "Mallor will still be here tomorrow after we win this!"

His encouraging words were met with quiet cheers, and it was clear very few of them could hide their excitement of being reunited. The anticipation of the night, however, showed.

The men were prepared. Each of them were well fed from Leon's packed food and well rested with the extra day they had. While it didn't give them a lot of time, Mallor knew just a few extra hours of rest with the clan meant the world. He felt guilty for the sleep he had gotten while living in luxury at Analise's, but now was not the time to pity himself.

They began climbing down the hill in small waves. Crouching the whole way to not be seen, the descent was slow. The silence would have been deafening, but the shouts from the stadium below gave them a bit of leeway. Regardless, the hunters held their breath. The tension was clear, and deep breaths of peace would not occur no matter how much noise there was around them. Mallor's thoughts, however, occupied the quiet.

As they neared the fighting arena, his breath was taken away by the enormity of the event. None of the men had seen the Election in their lifetime, and it was hoped by the witches the Election would never have to occur again after the Original Witch had been chosen.

The noise coming out of the arena was in stark contrast to the silence he spent the last half an hour in. He was overjoyed they seemed so occupied, knowing while they expected hunters in the vicinity, they did not anticipate this many. Mallor's clan had kept quiet and had chosen a path many assumed would take too long to make it to the Election. While Election security had kept an eye out for months, they didn't realize how fast the hunters were. No one knew what happened in hunter training, and the men moved strategically and with a speed many did not think humans could achieve. They were here, and no one knew.

Analise knew. She only knew Mallor was here, however. She welcomed him, and he missed her dearly. He couldn't wait for her to be overjoyed by the end of Cinder, and while he was anticipating a fight larger than life for his attempt at full massacre, he hoped she would see this as him protecting her against everything she hated about herself.

Shouts blared from families encouraging their witches to win. The fight was set up like Roman gladiators in the Colosseum. The names for the battle had been announced earlier that night and a scoreboard listed each name in bright lights. The stadium was massive, bustling with stands of families like any other sports game. Except they all knew this was no game. He worried, tossing over the fact he had been kept in the dark about how Analise intended to have her name read by the ballot, but he had full faith she would figure it out.

The fighting had long since begun, and the first Election had only lasted an hour. While each witch trained for months in this battle, there were few rules. Anything was fair game, and this was clear in how quickly the witches dropped like flies.

The scoreboard hanging at the top of the arena showed three witches were dead. Mallor read through the names quickly, scanning to ensure Analise's name wouldn't be there. It hadn't crossed his mind she could die during this fight, and he realized he was so concerned with protecting her from his own people he didn't realize she could be killed by her own. He pushed the thought aside, dismissing it as silly as he breathed a deep sigh of relief when her name was not on the "out of play" side of the board.

Three witches dead. That left six. The hunters needed two more to die before they could attack. Cell told him to attack when four were left was the best idea. They would shut the lights of the arena off, hoping an emergency siren would drive the bulk of the spectators out of fighting distance. Typically, this worked. Witches were powerful, but magic could backfire immensely. A sign to get out of the most dangerous fight they ever seen would not be abnormal. Faidor left early, and he would pull the alarm once Cell signaled to him it was time.

Another alarm bell rang, and a fourth witch was down. They couldn't see the fighting from where they were, and Mallor was almost thankful they couldn't. The men knew what the witches were capable of, but they didn't know everything Mallor did. Many of them carried them with more cruelty than Lilith. This meant they were unstoppable when angry, and the men needed to believe they were fighting against an enemy who they knew everything about. They would expect the unexpected as all fighters were taught, but they didn't need to know how real the unexpected was.

Just ten minutes later, the clock ticked away and one more name was added to the list.

The fifth witch was down. The alarm blared.

CHAPTER 30

———

The scattering sound of the witches was music to Mallor's ears. They fled the stadium like ants about to be stepped on, and the sight was an exhilarating thing. The men were loud in their cheers, no longer having to disguise their joy in quiet whispers and nod. Then, men in black training clothes with smiles bigger than anyone had ever seen, ran into the night.

They approached the arena and saw the fighting continued in flashes of movement.

Before his eyes, he saw Analise demolishing each of the women in front of her. She wore purple, the same color he first saw her in when he visited her office. Her eyes glowed green, and despite how little time he had to admire her in her stillness, he was taken.

Four witches remained in the arena, and most of the stands had emptied. The alarm had clearly phased many of the witches, but Analise continued to push them against each other, quickly teleporting away from any retaliation. Using her strength to put a witch in the place she stood in one second ago, she dodged defensive spells by letting someone else take the hit for her.

She dashed around, too fast for the witches to keep up with. He had never realized how good she was at teleportation and thanked his luck she was the one to teach him. She was now in the far-right corner of the arena, catching her breath as two witches brawled and a third laid on the ground nursing a wound.

The men stood on the sidelines, each waiting for the moment every witch lay in weakness to attack. While it was usually considered rude to attack an opponent when they were down, the idea of no rules or etiquette applied to the hunters too so far as they were concerned.

Analise had few seconds to sort her next move out, as the witches from four other clans, including Cinder, remained. The witch from Kent, named Millie, leapt through the air across the arena and took her wand to Analise's throat, wielding it like a knife. Mallor flinched but watched in awe as Analise used brute force to flip Millie over and snap her wand in two. Another witch whose name Mallor couldn't remember used a gust of wind to bring Analise to the center of the arena. They looked like they had teamed up against Analise and sought to cut off her hand. Mallor knew how hard it was to take Analise's hand and was grateful he hadn't done it in a devastating way all those years ago. Analise fought with grace, not a care in the world for the alliance that sought to rid her of power entirely.

She jumped through the air, kicking them both and using a final spell to set them into the ground with a large thud.

Each of the three witches were still alive, but as far as the hunters knew, this was the moment in which they would all be at their weakest. Analise looked out from the arena, making eye contact with Mallor as he peeked up from behind one of the seats. She smiled at him and nodded her head to indicate that now was his time.

"On them!" Mallor shouted out, a rush of pride filling his heart as his beautiful loved one indicated to him the fighting was allowed. Analise didn't know the hunters were there, but she knew for now they had a mission to accomplish. He swung into the arena, the hunters rushing in after him.

Faidor placed the dome around the arena, trapping everyone inside. This was the plan. The arena dome existed for rain to keep the stadium safe during the days of set up. Faidor was behind the scenes, using the controls of the arena to their advantage.

Now, it was just the hunters and the witches remaining in the Election. It was their time, fighting what would hopefully be their last fight ever.

———

The turf of the arena gave Mallor the advantage of speed, and when combined with barreling down the stadium at full capacity, there was no stopping him. The witches in the arena tried to stand up, but Analise kept striking them down. She reached for their hands, trying to get her spells to cut them off. Many of them wore protective bracelets, keeping any spells or charms from reaching their dominant hands. The only way to rid them of magic was to remove the bands by hand and cast a spell. Analise was preoccupied trying to keep them down to stop them from teleporting. No one could teleport out of the arena according to the charms and rules of the Election, but they could teleport all around within.

Mallor and the men dogpiled the witches, screaming in pain as they were singed by fire through defensive spells. They had trained for this, each of them being forced to undergo electric shocks nearly every day for the last six months to prepare for this moment. Fire from the witches itself felt unusually hot, and when paired with the witches' clear anger, the pain was searing. The smell of burning bodies ran strong, but the job of the Court as many of the men dedicated their lives to keeping the witches physically down was to remove any charmed bracelets. Mallor wanted so badly to use magic and strike the bands off, but he knew he couldn't expose himself.

He had no idea what would happen with the clan and Analise after this, and this was not the time to figure it out.

"Mallor!"

Analise shouted at him from the other side of the arena. A witch from one of the other covens had her in a chokehold, and Analise was starting to look weaker. Her legs looked weak, and her face was going red, meaning she had no physical capacity to cast a spell and move away. He ran to her but was stopped by Millie from the Kent coven. Millie was dogpiled but grabbed Mallor's ankle and yanked him to the ground. He struggled and reached for his knife to cut off her hand.

The witch struggled as he felt the tip of his knife go through the skin on her hand. His knife was knocked away as the witch in the other dogpile cast her hand at him. Analise's coughing was all Mallor heard as he felt his vision go blurry. He needed to get to her, and he needed to do it now. Otherwise, they would both die the sad death that came with suffocation.

He shut his eyes, thought of waking up next to her, and visualized being on top of the witch from Kent. He felt himself slip away from the grip of Millie and felt the gasps on the field as Mallor disappeared and reappeared on the shoulders of the Kent witch.

He took his wand, stuck it to her throat, and split open her neck as if it were the targets in the training room. She fell to the ground, her headless body collapsing to the floor.

Analise coughed loudly, catching her breath. "Thank you. Hunters?"

"No time right now. They're on our side." Mallor caught his breath, trying not to think about the magic he had performed in front of men who despised magical beings. "We need to go—now."

"I'll get Millie. She's done nothing but piss me off since the first day I met her."

"Good." Mallor gave her a quick wink, knowing nothing would make up for the kiss he wanted so desperately to plant on her.

The two ran into the middle of the area, Mallor reaching for the pile of men burning away and struggling to keep a witch from escaping the weight of the men. He struck her bracelet and cut off her hand.

He was shocked by how fast it all happened but made it his immediate goal to take the men off her and beat down the fire that was growing even with her death.

The whole arena smelled like burning dead bodies, and Mallor had to hold his breath to keep from vomiting as he yanked the men from the pile.

He heard struggle from behind him but knew Analise was quarrelling with Millie. The two were the last remaining witches, and although Mallor knew Analise would win, he also knew it wouldn't be easy.

A ringing began in his head once he saw Tate in the pile. His hair had been singed, and his arms were bright red as third degree burns developed. He had no idea how to cool the arm because he had no idea about spells beyond the two he really knew well.

There was no water in the area, and he had no idea how to help Tate. Tate was losing consciousness, going into shock right in front of Mallor's eyes. He was losing his closest friend, and he couldn't make it stop. It was then he realized, with all of the power he had as a leader and wizard, he couldn't stop himself from feeling loss.

He pulled Tate out of the pile, laying all of the men across the turf. He would return to them soon, but shut his eyes to try and teleport Tate out of the arena and into a cold shower. He was sure that it would work. It *had to* work.

The desperation Mallor felt to save Tate rivaled nothing, and he continued to try and push the ringing in his head away to focus on saving him.

The ringing was interrupted by a loud yell from a female voice. Mallor turned around, relieved to see Millie dead.

He looked around the room, hoping to find Analise and beckon her over. Now she had killed Millie, maybe she could help save Tate.

His heart stopped when he couldn't find her. He dropped Tate's hand, frantically scouring the stadium, praying he would find a purple speck somewhere. Maybe she was hiding? She had to be here. She couldn't leave the arena, not while the Election continued. Right?

And then, he saw her.

At the very top of the stadium, in the highest row of the spectator seats, stood Cell. Blood mixed with sweat from a cut on his forehead, Cell's eyes were menacing.

His knife was to her throat, and Analise's hand was fully severed. There was nothing but blood dripping from her elbow down.

CHAPTER 31

——

He turned, looking at Tate. Tate was losing life in front of him. He looked back at Analise. She had lost her magic. She couldn't fight Cell. She would lose her life, too.

He was conflicted, caught between his two worlds. Being betrayed by the one he grew up in and drawn to the one he had fought against for so long, he had no idea where to go.

If he teleported to her, he could strike Cell and come back for Tate. He could do it. He could have both.

He refused to believe he had to choose.

He shut his eyes, looking forward to her, thinking about the house from the dream. He yearned for that moment right now. He felt himself shift, hearing Tate groan as he slowly felt the surroundings around him disappear. The ringing in his head continued, growing louder as he ended up right in front of Cell.

Cell had never looked so vicious.

"I knew you were one of them, Mallor."

"You promised. You promised she would stay alive."

"You only want her because she gave you power. She's kept you captive, Mallor." He spit onto the floor in disgust, pressing the knife into the soft skin of Analise's neck. She whimpered.

He had never seen her so weak, trying to get words out but incapable as tears ran down her cheeks.

"You promised you were a hunter. That was the promise you made to me the day you showed up in training. Look at you." Cell scowled.

"I am. Tate needs help, Cell," Mallor pleaded, hoping he would see some form of reason. "I need you there now." He was begging to a man he never expected to have to. His mind spun, unsure of whether he could convince Cell to help him or find a way to save Analise.

Failure. Failure. Failure. He was beating himself up inside, even more conflicted by the bad timing of his self-pity.

"Tate has been soft since day one. Let him be. This is the fight we knew we'd die for." Cell's statement was heartless, and there was clearly no room to counter him.

Mallor would try anyway. It was all he could do. "We don't have to."

Analise screamed as the knife went deeper into the skin. Cell smiled, savoring every moment as if this kill were the same as any other.

"Please!"

Mallor tried to strike him, shutting his eyes to find a negative emotion. Nothing happened. He tried again. Shaking, he was incapable of physically attacking Cell without ensuring Analise's death. Analise was losing consciousness, and he was forced to watch life leave her eyes just as he was with Tate. He would lose two of them in a day, and there was just about nothing he could do about it.

Cell's eyes widened, and he began turning purple. Mallor stood there confused, tears flowing down his face. He turned around to see what was causing fear to enter Cell's soul, he saw Lilith.

For the first time, he was relieved to see her. She smiled at him and pushed him to the side. Cell's eyes rolled back in his head, and his legs collapsed under him. He crumpled to the floor, and just as Mallor hoped to breathe a sigh of relief, Cell took his knife to Analise's chest on the way down.

"Stop! She's pregnant!" His least favorite witch shouted at the two of them.

Cell's eyes went wide. And he dropped the knife, and fully dropped to the floor. His heavy breathing stopped, and Mallor didn't need to check his pulse to know he was dead.

The ringing in Mallor's head stopped. The world went silent, and he was unsure how to process Lilith's news. He grabbed her by the shoulders, looking at her with daggers in his eyes. Anger seared through his body, feeling deeply unpleasant about everything she had ever done or said to him. "Tell me how you know. Tell me right now, Lilith."

Her eyes lit on fire, hearing her full name. "Don't ever call me that."

"Tell me *how you know*."

"I saw it, Mallor. There is a child in her future."

Before he could process, a knife came hurtling toward Analise. She was now crouching on the floor, continuing to sob and shake in shock. There was no moving her, and although he yearned to comfort her, he had no idea how to process the death and news around him.

He stood there, incapable of moving, and Lilith teleported away. The Election was over. The magical bounds of the arena were done. Analise was the last remaining witch with no way to use magic. Tate was dead. Cell was gone.

The knife rushed toward Analise's heart, and Mallor was too late to see it.

He reached, wishing he could move more quickly.

She looked up, her green eyes going wide as she saw the knife coming her way. With no way to move, she whispered, "We love you."

Mallor threw himself in front of her and just as the tip of the knife grazed his chest, he felt the world around him fall away. With no idea of whether he was dead or alive, he reached for her arm, and instead found a hand he didn't recognize.

He blinked his eyes open, the smell of rotting bodies gone, only to find himself in the arms of Teil.

TO BE CONTINUED.

ACKNOWLEDGMENTS

This year has been the hardest of my life. It has been filled with grief and strain, both fighting to drain my life of magic. Through my imagination, however, I found a little universe tucked in the back of my brain with characters I admired. These individuals, although entirely fictional, have provided me comfort. I am repeatedly blown away by the support I have received as I have taken characters I love and have given them entire stories. Whether on social media or in person, each person who has reached out has made my heart soar and my smile brighter.

Becoming a published author at nineteen years old is a journey I would have never dared dream of and one that would not have come true without all of your support.

Thank you first and foremost to my family for supporting me every step of the way. I want to specifically thank my grandparents, my parents, Hari Kaka, Bhargavi Aunty, Manisha Aunty, Harish Mama, Girish Mama, Kalyani Aunty, Aparna Aunty, Viju Aunty, Shiva Uncle, Nagamani Chadalavada, Yugandhar Uncle, Prerna Atha, Sunny Uncle, Malavika Aunty, Vimathi, Nandini, Lakshmi Aunty, Madhumathi Aunty, Jagadesh Uncle, little Malvika, Vyas Uncle, and Anu Vellore. I am so lucky to have so many family members to love.

To my cousins, Rohan Chaturvedula, Ananya Tanjore, Yash and Arjun Rao, I can't wait to see the big things you all will do. They say Indian families are always huge, but I never understood the power of that capacity until recently. Secondly, I have to thank the friends who sat with me as I wrote this book. Thank you Sydney Sobel, Carol Puthussery, and Ria Villait for sitting inside with me, sacrificing days exploring Scotland, to guide me through writer's block. You three saw me create this universe firsthand.

Thank you to Joshua Ramdass, Nicholas Rullo, Lacey Mathis, Iona Molland, Angelina Paul, Edwina Eyre, Jahnavi Prabahla, and Dean Satouri for picking up my endless Facetime calls. I am blessed to feel closer to you all with each passing day, despite living across the world.

Thank you to the friends from my childhood, namely Sarena Oberoi, Roma Sharma, Grace Crangle, Nikita Sajai, Jahnavi Chindepalli, Vibha Erasala, Daichi Monma, Antonia Pellegrini, Andreas Borgh, Eloah Makassi, Lily Gates, Anika Kumar, Allison Fowle, Savannah Sides, Sudiksha Kochi, Iyan Faruque, Sreenaina Koujala, Roy Hadden, Abby Dimmick, Adina Mobin, Jeff Chesson, Keita Heinrich, Andrew Otchere, Lucas Johnson and Thomas Jackson.

Thank you to my William and Mary family, namely Katherine Brewer, Alena Gartner, Marisa Lemma, Ana Suarez, Caitlyn Whitesell, Michael Jackson, Tarra Olfat, Sophie Halkett, Jonah Finkel, Lauryn Walker, Taiana James, Sunita Ganesh, Olivia Little, Jessie Henry, Rush Lee, Meghana Reddy Boojala, and Nicola Price.

I also have to thank my St. Andrews family, including Kiara Snyder, Lauriane Hughes, Isy Platt, Conor Sinnott, Julija Koletnik, Keyona Fazli, Catherine Cooper, Kirsty Peng, Reece McMahon, Ava Cordero, Sebastian Anderson, and

Emmanuella Ellia, for bringing me into a new school and supporting me through writing this book.

It is a beautiful thing to keep close to the individuals you have met throughout this journey. To the individuals who made each day brighter, both abroad and in the United States, I thank Padmaja Baru, Radhakrishnan, Hailee Eiker, Alexandra Armitage, Marli Watson, Vikrant Kothari, Marla Tobey, Elizabeth Parham, Mirja Gerloff, Sam Adams, Marta Westerstahl, Carmen Andrade, Amanda Burgess, Alexander Stach, Rosa Le, Isidora Bertrand, Ellie Ransom, Evie Thomas, Roy Hadden, Jackson McFadden, Esther Ignacio, Paulina Bomm, and Roland Ramdass. Thank you so much.

Lastly, thank you to the mentors and adults who I look up to. Thank you to Audrey Bell, Marisa Sprowls, Eric Koester, Charlotte McConnel, Bradley Burzumato, Jessica Berg, Benjamin Shewbridge, Hannah Arrighi, Brittany Ruyak, Lauren Gilbert, Sarah Campbell, Leslie Emery, Paul Lee, and Judy Ramdass for being the adults who believed in all of my crazy ideas.

Thank you to each and every one of you for preordering my book and supporting me. I am blessed to live this life, and I extend the utmost gratitude to each of you. You have all made me a published author as a first-generation American at nineteen years old. My life feels surreal thanks to your efforts.

Again, thank you.

Printed in Great Britain
by Amazon